A MOTHER'S INFLUENCE

Real struggles, adversity and tenacity

This is a work of fiction.

Names, characters, and incidents either are the product of the author's imagination or are used fictitiously. Any resemblance to actual person, living or dead, events, or locales is entirely coincidental.

Copyright 2015 by Willie Mae Gearing

Published in the United States

www.amothersinfluencenovel.com

ISBN# 978-0-692-44098-8

DEDICATION

This book is dedicated in honor of my parents, Bobby and Louise Gearing. They both instilled values in me and taught me to do my very best in life.   I thank them and GOD every day for giving me the courage and strength to set goals and accomplish my dreams. I am glad that my parents grounded me with a spiritual "foundation" so even when their voices were silent I still had something to hold on to.

Chapter One

I'm nearly home, but I don't recall much of my familiar route. I left work early, hopped in my car and the rest was a blur. I do recall it took an extra effort not to take a detour to the mall. While driving home, my eyes wandered to the rearview mirror and I caught a glimpse of my reflection. I was startled by the simple fact that my hair is so gray; twenty years have slipped by me. As I pulled into the driveway, I was overjoyed. After weeks of hard work, I could finally park my car in the garage. I sighed, as I realized I had more cleaning to do, but my first priority is the office.

When I bought this house ten years ago, it had four bedrooms and I knew I needed to turn one of the rooms into a home office. I can't remember the last time I had used my home office or given it a thorough cleaning. I had to get ready for Samantha, my best friend, to arrive. She was getting married in a few months. We had plans to relax with a glass of wine (or maybe a half glass for me) and search bridal magazines for Samantha's perfect wedding dress.

After parking the car, I rushed up the stairs, changed into my jeans, grabbed my dust rag and proceeded down the hall to the dust filled bookcase in my office. As I began to dust, I saw a picture of Ryan and a feeling of sadness instantly came over me.

I asked myself, what would life have been like with Ryan as my husband?

I was having a vivid image of our daughter saying, "Mama, can I watch TV?" I replied from the kitchen, "Jennifer, have you done your homework? Do your homework first, honey. As soon as Dad gets home, we're gonna have supper. Dad is checking on Grandma tonight. He has a few errands to run for her and I'd like for us to at least have supper together before he leaves."

A Mother's Influence

A few minutes later, I could hear the rumbling of the garage door. Ryan was home. As Ryan walked up to me, I felt him pull my hair aside and place gentle kisses on my neck.

"Hi honey, I thought about you a lot today."

"Oh, how sweet, you thought about me?"

"I noticed the article about your company having huge lay-offs when my secretary brought in the paper this morning."

A look of disappointment appeared on my face. "Ryan, didn't we just have this conversation? My company just got a new CEO and he's making a lot of changes. I survived the job cuts but I don't know how much longer that'll last. It's comforting to know you didn't take the job they offered you and that we aren't working for the same company."

Ryan left the room to wash up for dinner. A few minutes later, I yelled to Ryan and Jennifer that dinner was ready. It was a warm summer evening and I decided that we should eat on the screen porch. The magnolias were fragrant at this time of the year. We all sat down for supper and held hands, as Ryan said grace. He squeezed my hand gently before letting it go. "The lasagna looks delicious," he said. As he gazed and winked his eye at me, he said, "You always know what I have a taste for." It was his way of planting a thought about what he really wanted later that evening.

He always joked that my cooking rated up there with his mom's which was why he married me. Ryan looked at Jennifer and asked, "How's my little princess?"

Blushing, she said, "I'm good Daddy." At eight years old, she was looking more like her dad every day. She had his dimples and gorgeous smile. Ryan was a good looking man but that was never what caught my eye. He was the most sensitive and caring man I'd ever met. He always made time for his family. He was the son of a single mother and they looked after each other. He would consider her in all of his decisions, sometimes too much. The phone rang, startling me.

A Mother's Influence

I realized I'd been daydreaming. I ran down the hall to answer the phone. It was Samantha. She was just checking to see if I had gone straight home. I started to laugh. "Oh, you think I don't know my way home? I know I don't live at the mall." It had been a private joke between us because we spend so much time there. Finally, I said, "I'll see you when you get here."

I finished cleaning the office, somewhat satisfied with the results. The doorbell chimed, leaving me no time to change my mind. With one last wary look at the room, I went to answer the door.

Excited, Samantha came with bridal magazines in tow. I told her that I had purchased a few magazines, as well. We walked down the hall to the office and placed the magazines on the desk. We combed through the pile of bridal magazines until she found the perfect dress.

"This is the one!" she shouted.

I rushed over to see the dress that would end my misery. I felt slightly jealous of Samantha's way with men; something I could only daydream about.

"Let's celebrate," I said but inwardly I was longing to be in her shoes and have a man of my own. We were both happy that she had decided on the perfect dress. She was ready to leave after an exhausting evening because she had to get up early in the morning for her cake tasting.

After Samantha left, I decided to turn in. I figured the few sips of wine we had earlier would help me get to sleep. I tossed and turned, thinking about my life and feeling empty inside. I felt so alone without someone special. Most of my friends had husbands and children and I was alone. I glanced over at the clock and noticed it was two o'clock in the morning.

I had too much on my mind to sleep, so I got up. I went back into my office to put away the bridal magazines that

A Mother's Influence

I'd purchased. I moved a book on the shelf to make room for the magazines and the picture of Ryan fell on the floor again. I stared at that picture for a long time, reflecting on why Ryan and I hadn't gotten together all those years ago.

One day after school, I decided to take a walk around the Twin Oakes apartment complex, which was part of my neighborhood. We lived in one of those progressive communities that had townhomes, apartments and single family homes. I spotted a guy washing his canary yellow Volvo. I notice that he was about five feet nine, medium complexion, very muscular and wore a mustache.

As he glanced up at me, I could see he had a gorgeous smile and dimples. As I walked past, he was rinsing the suds off his car. He looked up at me, pointing the water hose in my direction. I jumped "I'm sorry, he said." "I wasn't trying to get you wet."

I said, "You should have tried harder."

My yellow dress got wet and he apologized. "You did that on purpose," I said.

He said, "I didn't." And with a smile, he introduced himself as Ryan.

I told him, "My name's Anolese and, by the way, you didn't have to get me wet to get my attention."

He said, "I've never seen you before. Where do you live?"

"It's for me to know and you to find out," I said, as I kept walking.

I found out from my cousin Wanda that Ryan and his mother had just moved into the apartment complex within the last two weeks. I later discovered that he had been asking around about me and had changed his jogging route so he could run past my house every day. His smile had attracted me to him. I wondered if I'd ever get the opportunity to know him better. He wasn't a high school student because I'd never seen him at school.

I later discovered from Jasmine, a girl at school who knew everybody's business, that Ryan had graduated from a high school in a nearby town and his mother had moved them here for a job opportunity.

Every day after school, I would sit on the glider on the front porch of my house and do my homework just to catch a glimpse of him running down the street. We would wave at each other, but he never stopped to talk. I found out that Ryan jogged three miles back and forth to the town square every day.

I had been trying to figure out the perfect place to run into him, when out of the blue, my mama said, "Anolese, I need for you to get off the school bus downtown and run a few errands for me." She didn't realize I was more than happy to run her errands. I knew about what time Ryan would be running, so I could get my errands done quickly and conveniently be walking home along his jogging path when he was there.

I was so busy looking for him that, in that moment, my hands were sweaty and I dropped my books. When I bent down to pick them up, he was staring at me. "May I?" he asked, and began picking up the rest of my books. My heart was beating so fast I could hardly get out the word, "okay." "Are you new here?" I nervously asked. "What brought you here?"

He said, "My mom just got a job."

"What kind of job? What does she do? Where does she work? What school did you graduate from?"

Ryan said, "Whoa, I'd rather not talk about me. I want to know more about you."

"Okay," I finally said, "you answer two of my questions and I'll answer two of yours

Deal?"

"Deal," Ryan said. "My mom is a nurse and works at the Presbyterian Hospital. I graduated from Jefferson High School and that's enough about me. Anolese, what grade are you in?"

"I'm a junior in high school."

"Oh," Ryan sighed, already calculating our age difference. He knew it was going to be a problem.

Ryan asked me about my hobbies and I told him I liked to read and decorate. I told him that I had a part time job babysitting and I used all my money redecorating my bedroom. "I know you probably think that's silly but I want to be a designer and a writer one day." Before he could say anything, I noticed we were down the street from my house. "I gotta go now," I said.

He handed me my bags. "I hope to see you again," he said and started to run away from me.

Walking home, I was on cloud nine: I couldn't feel the weight of the bags and the books I was carrying. When I got into the house, my mama asked me if I had any problems and I answered "No."

Mama said, "You have a strange look on your face." I said, "I'm okay, Mama. I'm going to go sit on the front porch and do my homework."

Still in a trance, thinking about my conversation with Ryan, I almost didn't hear my Mama say, "Anolese, you know it's Friday. You can put it off for one day."

Mama, "it's not a problem. I want to be able to do some fun things tomorrow." Saturdays consisted of getting up early, cleaning the house, helping out with the yard work, and maybe spending a few hours with my friends. This Saturday, doing homework was the furthest thing from my mind. Sunday was a

A Mother's Influence

day that we spent in church. I taught Sunday school for preschoolers and sang in our church choir. Sunday's didn't leave much time for anything else.

Mama always got us up early on Sunday mornings for a big breakfast, as we normally didn't get back home from church until three in the afternoon. Being with the preschoolers was more like working in daycare than teaching Sunday school, constantly dealing with their short attention spans. Sometimes, I couldn't wait for it to be over so that I could change into my choir robe and get ready to sing. The choir always marched into church together singing, "Welcome to Zion."

As I entered the choir stand and looked down at the audience, I spotted Ryan sitting with a woman who I presumed was his mother but looked more like his grandmother. This Sunday, my loud, high pitched voice was more reserved. I tried not to look at him, but I could feel him staring at me. I was so infatuated with him. Anxiously, I couldn't wait for the end of service, so I could get outside to talk with him before he left.

He was standing on the church steps off to the side. We waved at each other. "Do you mind if I walk you home?" He asked.

I said, "No." I went back into the church and told my mama I was leaving to walk home. "Okay," she said, "set the table for dinner when you get there."

"Okay," I said. Ryan and I walked slowly, chatting non-stop and were still standing outside the house when Mama and Dad came walking towards us. I introduced Ryan to them.

My parents were very polite and said, "Hello, young man." I knew from the look that mama gave me that it was time to say goodbye to Ryan. I went into the house and my mama said, "I think that young man and his mother just moved here and I was told that he graduated from high school a year or so ago. Anolese, if that's the case, he's much too old for you."

I said, "Mama, we were just having a conversation."

"About what?" she asked.

All I could come up with was, "Today's sermon. We were talking about the sermon and he is thinking about joining the choir." That was my first lie.

Mama made it clear that she did not want me hanging around with someone she considered an older man. I sat on the porch everyday after school to do my homework. Even if it was raining outside and some of the spray from the rain hitting the edge of the porch would get me wet I would watch Ryan jog or just daydream about what our lives would be like together. I had my future all mapped out. I knew I wanted to become his wife one day. I decided, since I knew my mama would never approve of me seeing Ryan that I would find other ways to be with him. I could babysit for Wanda's son, Seth, who lived in Twin Oakes apartments, knowing that Ryan lived just down the street.

I asked my mama if I could keep Wanda's son, my little cousin, this weekend and she agreed. She had no idea of the plan I was concocting. *Perhaps Ryan will see me as I play with my little cousin.*

Saturday came and just as expected, my plan worked perfectly. He saw me outside playing with my little cousin. He walked over and talked with me. Ryan said that he was taken by me; that I was unlike any girl he'd ever met. He began to talk about our age differences and said we could only be friends. "I realize that," I said, even though I wanted much more. I did not tell him about my mama and how she felt about him talking to me.

I eventually hung out with Ryan a lot more because he joined the choir.

A Mother's Influence

Sometimes, I would sneak out of the house and have secret encounters with him. He was always a gentleman. I was always cautious because I knew if we went too far-anything more than friends - it would be inappropriate due to our age difference. We would meet at the park and sometimes at my cousin Wanda's house, but we always had to be aware of the time; my mama worked and her shift ended at eleven. Mama had often told me that Ryan was a man and that I was still a little girl, which infuriated me. Mama said that a seventeen - year old girl should not be hanging around a twenty one - year old man.

At seventeen, I knew exactly what I wanted in my life; and it was Ryan. Ryan finally got up enough nerve to ask me if I would go to the movies with him. He kept reminding me that we were just two friends, hanging out. He had no idea that my mama was against us seeing each other. I told him that he could pick me up at seven but that we needed to be home by 10:30pm, because I needed to put the finishing touches on a project I was doing for school; it was another lie. Ryan and I had a great time. Our shoulders touched and, at one point, he had his arms around my chair, letting his arm gracefully caress my shoulders. As I turned to look at him, he kissed me on the cheek. I forgot all about the movie and just wanted to kiss him and put my head on his shoulder.

The next day, all I could think about was Ryan. When the teacher in my Science class called upon me to answer a question, I didn't even know what the question was. I asked him to repeat it. I was too busy thinking about seeing Ryan again.

Later that day while riding the school bus home, we drove through the apartment complex and I spotted Ryan's Volvo. I wondered what he did all day. My stop was next, and I mindlessly got off the bus and walked to my house. I got in the door, and dropped my books, got a glass of water and when mama said, "Anolese, can I see you in the living room?" My

A Mother's Influence

heart started to pound. She confronted me by saying, "I heard

some disturbing news. Anolese, did you leave the house last

night without asking?"

I raised my chin and without hesitation stated loudly,

"Yea, I did!" I felt like I was going to explode. My voice had

reached a tone that even frightened me. I told her that I went

to the movies with Ryan.

"You did what?" she said. "How dare you defy me? I

told you not to hang around that man."

I told my mama she couldn't possibly understand the

love I had for him, - that she was too old to understand.

My mama said, "What did you say?" I could see the

anger rising in her. Her face had become distorted. Visibly

shaking, she picked up a broom and raised it to hit me. I could

see the broom coming down on me when I raised my hand to

grab it before it could hit me.

I jerked the broom from my mother's hand. I walked to the far end of the room and placed the broom in the corner. I looked back at my mother and, without saying anything, shot her another glance that said, "You ain't gonna hit me with no broom, sister."

Mama yelled at me, "You act too grown; too big for your britches. Out of all of my children, you're the most disrespectful. You're smelling yourself, girl! I'll ring your neck! I brought you into this world and I'll take you out." She walked toward me with her finger pointing directly at my face. "Don't you ever raise your hand to me again!!!" She warned.

I hadn't raised my hand to strike her. I would never do that. At that moment, I could see tears forming in her eyes and realized how disappointed my mother was in me for snatching the broom away from her; standing up to her and defying her. A look of confusion came over her. I think my mama was witnessing how her little girl was growing up and desiring to make her own decisions.

Mama realized I was fearlessly defending my position about Ryan. But I still felt that she didn't understand what I was feeling for him, - I loved him. I wanted to marry him and most of all I wanted to spend the rest of my life with him. I dreamed of having his baby, a little girl we would name Jennifer. I thought, it was a dream that seemed so distant. *But none of those things will ever come to pass,* as mama reiterated that I was not to see him again.

I tried to figure out how she found out that I'd sneaked out of the house that night. The next day, I overheard a conversation my parents were having. Mama told Dad what had happened. She said the neighbor had seen Ryan pick me up in a yellow Volvo and dropped me off several hours later. I thought, *why doesn't our neighbor have a life of her own? Why did she have to meddle in mine?*

Later, that same day, both my parents sat me down to lay down the law. I was told that I couldn't leave the house except for school and church; I couldn't talk on the phone to anyone. I even had to stay in my room and not go outside after school to talk with my friends. I was on a two month lockdown. I didn't know how I was going to survive. Ryan and I couldn't see each other anymore. *How am I going to tell him about my punishment?*

The next day, Mama didn't come straight home from work. She called and my sister answered the phone. My sister stared down at me when she was off the phone. "You're in trouble, "she said, Mama went to have a chat with Ryan's mom." I thought about running away from home, but where would I go? I had always been able to think through situations and I didn't know what the punishment would be if I left home or even if they'd allow me to come back. I was sure Ryan knew I was on punishment; Mama took care of that.

A Mother's Influence

I had to pass the neighbor's house every day, the one who had told on me. I used to say to myself, *I hope she chokes on the snuff she is dipping.* All she did was sit on her porch or peek through her blinds watching every move I made. I told myself, *I'll get her back at Halloween by throwing eggs at her house.* But who was I kidding? Where would I get the eggs? It was a stupid idea and I knew I would never go through with it, but it was a comforting thought.

It was a grueling two months. I couldn't even talk to my friends on the phone. During my punishment, it was pretty much school, home and church. I didn't even get to babysit anymore.

After my punishment finally ended, my parents would occasionally let me babysit for Wanda's son, who lived near Ryan's house. I felt like I was back in business and I would sneak around and have chats with Ryan. He had found out from his mother how my parents felt and his mother told him to leave me alone and never see me again.

Ryan told me that he cared deeply for me. He continued to say I was different from the other girls he'd dated. He told me I was fun to be around. He said I was head strong, smart and witty. Ryan said he enjoyed our conversation. He mentioned how hard it was for him not to see me.

Ryan grew up without a dad and was basically a mama's boy. He told me he did not want to continue to deceive his mother, - that he couldn't be in the same town with me and not be with - me even as his friend. He said he had gone down to the military recruiting office and was considering joining the Marines.

I began to cry and begged him not to make any rash decisions. I told him that somehow, we would be together. He said after my mama had the conversation with his mother, every time he left the house his mother would say, "Ryan, you aren't sneaking around to see that Anolese girl, are you?" He said, "No," mother.

Ryan said, "Anolese, I don't think I have a choice. I can't lie to her and sneak around seeing you. My only other choice is to leave. I don't feel the same way about anyone else but you."

I saw Ryan a few weeks later on the jogging path and he told me that he had made up his mind to join the Marines and had signed the papers and would be leaving in the next twenty days. He told me he wanted to be able to tell me goodbye and see me one last time. I was trying to plot and plan how to make that happen.

I decided to become the model child and do things around the house so that I could spend the night with one of my friends who seemed to have more privileges than I had. My girlfriend, Susan, had her own car. Susan asked me if I wanted to spend the weekend with her and that she would help me see Ryan one last time. I remembered the day Susan's mama called my house to see if I could spend the weekend with them.

After several minutes on the phone, my mama finally agreed; from Friday night to Sunday, but said I was to be in church on Sunday morning. I heard parts of their conversation, but mama walked into my room to tell me what she'd agreed to. All I really wanted was just a sleepover with my girlfriend, but the entire weekend was a bonus.

I called Ryan when I knew his mom would be at work and told him of my plans. That Friday night, Susan's mother went on a date and Susan and I were left at home to watch movies and eat popcorn. Susan had plans of her own for the evening and we had agreed to meet back at her mom's house at a certain time. We hoped that no one would ever find out what we had planned. Ryan showed up about an hour after Susan's mom left. We wanted to make sure Susan's mom didn't forget something and had to come back to the house. When Ryan arrived, I went out to greet him. I didn't want him to disrespect their home by coming in. I knew if someone found out, I would be in enough trouble.

We went for a drive but, not to risk being seen together, we were only going to be away from the house for one hour. It was the best hour of my life. We were able to talk and hold each other's hand and share a few kisses that made me melt inside. Hugs that tenderly caressed our touching bodies, I felt loved and he told me he loved me. I wanted everything he was willing to give. I had feelings I had never experienced before. My mind was filled with anticipation.

Being with Ryan had created senses I didn't know I was able to experience. As I rested my head on his chest, I could feel his heart pounding. I could tell he was just as excited to be with me. Ryan stated he was trying to control his mind and fight back all of his emotions. He did not want to lose control of himself. Ryan was a gentleman. "Anolese, we need to slow down," he said.

I knew he was the kind of person I would love and respect for the rest of my life. From that day on, I knew Ryan would always have my heart.

He promised me he would try to keep in touch somehow. I didn't have much faith in those words but I said okay. I realized after Ryan dropped me off at Susan's house that we were seeing each other for the last time. I couldn't think about, - let alone imagine - spending the summer without him.

Months went by and all I could think about was, *how will my life turn out? Where will I go from here - What would I become in the future?* Summer vacation was almost over but it was still very hot. We didn't have central air. All we had were a few room air conditioners -one in the bedroom and one in the living room. I was tired of being cooped up in the house, so I decided to go sit on the front porch. At one time, it was my favorite place. I would stretch out on the yellow glider and read a book.

Today, I just needed to be outside for a change of scenery and to pretend I was reading so I could people watch.

My mama joined me and said, "Anolese, we need to go back in the house. It is just too hot out here" I looked up and the mail truck was approaching our house.

The mail lady waved and spoke to my mama, saying, "It's so hot today I could have cooked my breakfast on the sidewalk."

My mama started to laugh and said, "I know what you mean."

Mama told me to go in the house and get a cold glass of lemonade and put it in a 'to go' cup, so the mail lady could take it with her. When I returned with her lemonade, she had gotten out of the truck and was handing the mail to Mama. I could see a white envelope trimmed in red and blue and I knew it was from the military. At that time, my brother was also in the Marines, stationed overseas. I watched my mother's face, as she looked down at the envelope with much anticipation. She had a puzzling look on her face.

I had a feeling the letter was not from my brother, but from Ryan. As Mama held the letter, I wondered if she was trying to decide whether or not to give it to me. I was surprised when she handed the letter to me without saying a word. This was my first letter from Ryan. From that day on, I greeted the mail lady. I must have read his letters a thousand times. His first letter didn't say much - only that he had finished basic training and how much he missed me. He told me he would be home soon before being shipped overseas. I couldn't wait until he came home, even though it was just for a short while and I was hoping to see him. I don't know if my mama found the letter and read it and knew what day he would

A Mother's Influence

be home or not, because we were conveniently visiting

relatives a few towns away. I never got to see him. I wrote

back to Ryan and told him what had happened. I told him that

I believed my mama took me away on purpose. I didn't get

another letter from him, but I remained hopeful.

In the fall, I started my last year of high school. When

I started school, the first thing I would do every day when I got

home was to look on the kitchen counter to see if I had a letter

from Ryan. Most days, there was no mail for me.

Chapter 2

I was a senior in high school, well liked by my teachers and the school staff. Surprisingly, my love for Ryan did not affect my focus on doing my school work. I was determined to do my very best in school. I kept my grades up because I wanted to go to college. I tried to keep myself active by playing in the marching and concert bands, and singing in the glee club. I enjoyed taking trips to other schools for football games and year end concerts.

In many ways, singing in the church choir, prepared me for the auditions. I loved to cook and Home Economic classes taught me additional skills. I had a few close girlfriends, but guys did not interest me. I had already met my one true love and, at times, the separation was more than I could bear.

During the beginning of the school year, dances and student parties did not interest me. Even if I felt I had to attend a function, I always went alone. I didn't want to be with anyone else but Ryan. I attended most of my school functions alone. I got a part-time job so I could pay for some of my graduation supplies such as my yearbook, class ring and my cap and gown. Ryan and I both shared that independent trait earning our own way, so we could make our own decisions and be on our own one day. I worked every Saturday afternoon at the same place where Ryan's mother worked. We would pass each other in the break room and I would listen from afar as she told stories about Ryan. She would graciously answer any questions I asked about him. His mother just dismissed my interest as total infatuation for her son. In contrast, when my mother caught me reading one of Ryan's letters, she would reiterate, "You need to stop thinking about that man," and "I hope you are not waiting for him because you will never be able to date him as long as you are living under my roof." Mama was very concerned about our relationship because I would soon be of legal age.

A Mother's Influence

Though I missed Ryan dearly, I did not want to miss the Senior Prom. Everyone was talking about the prom and getting excited about the class picnic. In my mind, I felt that if I attended any of the class events with someone, I would be unfaithful to Ryan - even though I could have gone with my girlfriends.

I decided to write Ryan a letter telling him what I was feeling. It was so hard to sort through my feelings and write about them at the same time. It took me several days to write a paragraph. I could barely get through the letter without shedding tears. I worked on the letter when no one was around because I didn't want anyone to see or know of my heartache. I told Ryan we would both be better off if we went our separate ways. Mama was never going to approve of him because of our age difference. I was still her little girl and, in Mama's eyes, too young to be in a serious relationship.

A Mother's Influence

A few weeks later, I received what would be my last letter from Ryan. He told me he understood how I felt, but he wanted me to know he would always love me. Ryan told me he had had some rough days in boot camp but my letter felt as if he had been kicked in the gut. He professed his love to me and told me that if this is what I wanted, he would reluctantly stop trying to wait out the time for us to be together. I went through several weeks of grieving. A loss is a loss, no matter how you look at it, and I needed to mourn my separation from Ryan.

I finally started to attend pep rallies and basketball games with my friends. After several weeks of hanging out with the rest of my classmates, I was asked out to the prom. Billy was a handsome young man from a nice family and my parents liked him. I explained to Billy that I thought of him as a friend and for him not to get any other ideas. My parents were pleased that, after all this time, I had a date for the prom. Billy took me to most of my senior events. My mama was thrilled to help me pick out a prom dress. I didn't want the usual long formal gown. I chose a short, cocktail type, hot pink laced dress that was fitted and showed off all my curves.

When Billy picked me up, he said, "Anolese, wow, you look great! I picked the right color flower without even knowing." Billy continued to say, "You look great. Let me pin the flower on you."

My mama looked at Billy, took the flower and pinned it on my dress. She took several pictures of Billy and me, and a few with my dad. Billy volunteered to take a picture of me with my parents.

As we started to leave, my father used his hand to press down on Billy's shoulder. "Young man," he said in a stern voice, "take care of my daughter, go straight to the dance and be in by midnight." My father never took his eyes off Billy when he uttered those words.

Mama just said, "Drive safely and have a good time."

A Mother's Influence

As we went out the door, Billy looked at me and said, "Your dad meant what he said. I saw it in his eyes."

I said, "Yeah, Dad is very protective, but let's just have fun."

As we pulled up to the school gymnasium, there was valet parking. Billy came around and opened the door for me. He grabbed my hand and walked me past the crowd. I felt like a princess on the arm of my Prince Charming. I knew it was going to be a magical night. I couldn't wait to get into the gymnasium. The smelly gym had been transformed into a "Night in Paris." The only fear I had was that I was not a good dancer. I just wanted to show off my dress. I looked around the room and my classmates no longer looked like kids. Dressed in our finest attire, we all looked like grown adults.

The tables were decorated beautifully; a replica of the Eiffel tower and a bouquet was placed in the center of each table. There were several cardboard standees of the Eiffel tower placed throughout the area. It no longer looked like a gymnasium with all the flowers, lights and decorations. It was magnificent. I was taken in by the beauty of the magnolias when I spotted the arch where I couldn't wait for Billy and me to take pictures. The smells of magnolias were in the air. I was so glad I had come to the prom; I just wish I had been there with the man I loved and not Billy. I didn't want to disappoint Billy by being ungrateful that he was the one I was with. I tried to have fun and I let him kiss me on the cheek a few times. I could tell he was having a good time because every time I looked over at him, he was gazing at me with a smile on his face - like I was the most beautiful girl in the room.

Thirty minutes before midnight, Billy and I left the prom. I didn't' live that far away and we had just enough time to stop at Burger Chef and get a cheeseburger before he took me home. We just made it to my house before midnight. Billy walked me to the door. I asked him if he wanted to come in for

A Mother's Influence

a few minutes. My parents were still up. I knew they were

waiting to see if I got home on time. They were in the living

room watching a movie when Billy and I went into the dining

room to eat our burgers. I told Billy I had a great time and that

he was a perfect gentleman.

As I walked him to the door thirty minutes later, he said

he had a great time and asked me if we could see each other

again. I reminded him that we were only friends. I didn't want

to lead him on because I didn't have the same feelings for him

that I had had for Ryan - and never would.

I was looking forward to graduation. However, it was

somewhat melancholy. I looked forward to keeping in touch

with a few of my classmates that had become friends for life. I

knew that I would never see the rest of my classmates and

teachers again and sadness came over me. It would be the first

of many changes in my life that I would just have to deal with.

Graduating from high school was the most exciting day of my life and I did so with honors. I was ranked number ten in a graduating class of two hundred fifty students. As I walked across the stage to get my diploma, I could hear the screams from my parents and friends. For a brief moment, I looked around at the place that I would never see again. I was overwhelmed with joy and sadness, as I could see from the tears of my classmates they must have felt the same way. At that moment, I felt the diploma represented my passage into adulthood. I had already been accepted at Reinhardt College, a junior college close to home, because I wanted some time to decide on my major and career goals. This would also ease the financial burden my parents would take on for me.

After the graduation ceremony, I could see Billy standing with my parents. But my eyes went toward my father's face. He had an expression that I had never seen before. Dad said with tears welled up in his eyes, "Anolese, I'm so proud of you for graduating tenth in your class. You know that I never had the chance to graduate from high school. I had to leave school in the fourth grade to help take care of my family. You've made me so proud. I felt like I was walking across the stage with you."

I tried not to look directly into Dad's eyes because I knew I would have cried.

My mama grabbed me and held me so tight. I knew that every memory she had of me was flashing through her mind. At that moment, she knew that life had changed for all of us. My grandparents were sitting patiently, looking at what was taking place. I went over and hugged them and told them they were the reason that I had accomplished so much and that I was sharing this day with them. I told my grandparents that I loved them and gave them both a kiss. I could see Billy waiting patiently for his turn.

As he walked over to me, Billy knew that this day would probably be the last day he would see me. He and his parents were spending the summer abroad. Billy came over and said, "We did it, Anolese, we made it; don't forget my graduation party starts at seven."

"I'll be there," I said.

Mama had planned a small celebration with relatives. I couldn't wait to get home to open my graduation gifts. As I walked toward the door, I could smell the aromas and I knew Mama had cooked all of my favorites just for me. After the celebration with my family, I told my parents, "Thank you for everything. I appreciate the values that you've instilled in me and I hope to always make you proud of me." I left the house to go to Billy's party.

When I woke up the next morning, Dad and Mama were looking excited. Dad said to me, "Anolese, we have a surprise for you." My dad handed me a set of keys to a car and said it was parked outside. Dad said, "It's not much, but it'll get you back and forth to school."

A Mother's Influence

I was overjoyed. I didn't care about the make and model. I was just happy to have a car.

During my first semester, I made the honor roll. I think I just wanted to make sure I would pass my college courses. My name appeared in the local paper and I was pleased with my accomplishments. The college I attended always put the names of their students who made the honor roll in the newspaper. My parents and grandparents were very proud of me. My parents bought several copies of the paper, had the article framed and hung it up on display. They mailed the remaining copies to other family members.

I continued my part-time job at the hospital, where I learned that Ryan had been honorably discharged and had enrolled in college out of state. *It seems he'd gone on with his life without me,* I thought I had to tell myself, *It's time for you to do the same thing.*

A Mother's Influence

As much as I liked being in college, I was looking forward to my summer vacation. I knew my parents had plans to send me and my little sister to spend the summer with my older sister in Buffalo, New York. I couldn't wait to leave our little small town of Canton, Georgia and experience a bigger city. I had secretly made up in my mind that I was never going to return. It was time to start life away from home. Yes, I was running from home, wishing to be away from my mother, who I never forgave for ruining my relationship with Ryan, the true love of my life. *If only she'd let me be with the only man I ever loved and still love today.* I needed to get out from under her roof.

I had only been out of the state of Georgia twice; once to a wedding in South Carolina, and once to Alabama when my parents took my older sister to college. After my sister finished college, she married and moved to Buffalo. When I visited her, I truly enjoyed my freedom and the change of scenery. I told my sister I was going to apply for a summer job

A Mother's Influence

in Buffalo and, to my surprise, I got a job at a company called Quick Flash as a personal assistant in a temporary position in several departments for many different managers. I was able to show off my organizational and multi-tasking skills. The work was tedious, demanding but also quite rewarding. I screened calls and talked with employees before passing them off to higher level managers.

For the most part, my managers hardly ever had to intervene because I was so interested in the work and the growth opportunities. I was like a sponge, soaking it all in to be the best at whatever I was asked to do. I was making more money than my part-time job at the Presbyterian Hospital in Georgia and meeting new people. At Quick Flash, I was exposed to a corporate world of people who were engineers, chemists, scientists, lawyers, business professionals and so many others. They were people in careers I had never even considered. My job exposed me to so many different personalities.

I loved the interaction of the job, which helped me grow as an individual. I had begun to make a few friends. Elisa was tall and always had a smile on her face. I really don't think she ever had a bad day. Samantha had also moved to Buffalo to find work away from a small town. We both wanted to create better opportunities for ourselves. Samantha and I became exceptionally close because our office cubicles were directly across from each other and we had so much in common. We started work for Quick Flash on the same day. We were the same age and we had some of the same interests in life.

Most days, Samantha and I would have lunch together in the cafeteria but Elisa would eat at her desk. After about six months, Samantha noticed this guy checking me out, but he would never say anything to me.

After several weeks, he spoke. "Hello, I'm Ken Jones. And you are?"

"Anolese Turner."

A Mother's Influence

"I have been watching you for several weeks. You don't have a ring on your finger. Are you married? Are you dating anyone?"

"You're pretty direct, aren't you?"

"I'm an attorney, he said." We always try to get to the point. Why waste time when you see someone who interests you?"

"I'm not in court, so you need to find other ways to get your questions answered."

A few weeks later, I was sitting at my desk and the phone rang. It was Ken Jones.

"It took me a while, but I found other ways to get those questions answered," he said. "I was happy to find out that you're not married. I would still like to know if you're in a relationship because if not, I would like to take you out to dinner."

I just ignored Ken for a few weeks. I was too busy dealing with my parents and their disappointment in me for not returning back to Georgia after my summer vacation. I explained to my parents that I'd found a job and would still be able to continue my education. I was making more money than I had ever made and I was old enough to be on my own. I had made a decision not to go back and I know that whatever happened in my life, I would have to live with the consequences of my actions. I was enjoying my newfound freedom.

My parents were very upset, but I told them that I was old enough to make my own decisions. My little sister had to go home because she was much younger than me. Also, I knew my college education was also a strain on them. I felt liberated and excited to be on my own. I perceived this job would open up different possibilities for me as long as I continued my education. I decided it was time for me to make a life for myself apart from the man I still loved and desired.

A Mother's Influence

After a few months of saving money, I finally had enough to move into my own apartment. I moved into my own apartment and enjoyed my newly - found independence. I made just enough money to pay my rent and utilities. I saved what I could, but it wasn't enough to go back to college right away.

I often talked with my friends from home. They would keep me abreast of what was going on with Ryan. I knew when he got out of the Marines, when he bought a new car and who he was dating. I didn't try to contact him because I didn't want to upset my parents who would see this action as total defiance. Ryan had yet to contact me. I'm sure he didn't want to call my parents to find out any information, after my mother had had a conversation with his mother.

A year went by before the next time one of my friends contacted me for the sole purpose of passing on information about Ryan. I told them I didn't want to hear about him ever again. I finally said, "Who cares." We had both made choices that we had to live with. The last thing I heard was that Ryan had gotten married. I knew that it was done, finally over.

Weeks later, I saw Ken Jones in the cafeteria again. He asked me if I was dating anyone. He also said, "I like your accent. Where are you from?"

I told him that I was from Canton, Georgia and that I was not dating anyone.

He said, "I really would like to continue this conversation. Can I call you?"

I said, "Do you have anything to hide? Are you married? Do you have a girlfriend?"

He said, "No."

I said, "Why don't I call you?"

He gave me his phone number and said, "Call me anytime."

A Mother's Influence

That evening, I called Ken just to see who would answer the phone. He answered and we talked for hours. We made plans to have lunch together the next day. I told Samantha as soon as I got to work about the details of the conversation and the fact that Ken had asked me to have lunch with him. During our lunch together, he asked me out on a date. We decided to go to a movie. Being new in Buffalo with very little to do and not having any male friends, I said yes. We went out frequently. I spent most of my free time with him. We took long motorcycle rides on his Harley which he nicknamed Taz, short for "Tasmanian Devil." It took some getting used to because I had never been on a motorcycle. We went to parties together and enjoyed our frequent picnics on the beach. He would always pack a bottle of wine, cheese and crackers. I wasn't much of a drinker. A couple sips of wine were two sips too many for me. Sometimes, we would be at the beach until the sun went down.

I remember one day when he came to my apartment early in the morning to pick me up so we could enjoy the sunrise on the beach. We then went out for breakfast. I was often at

his apartment. I looked for signs of other women and there were

none that I could detect. Every couple of weeks, he would go

home to visit his parents in Chicago. After a year of being with

him, I thought I was in love again. He knew my most important

secret. I was a virgin. We talked about getting married. He

would always ask me, "If I asked you to marry me, would you?"

I would say, "Yes, yes of course. I think we're good

together and I can see a future with you."

Ken's looks reminded me of Ryan. Ken met my parents

when they came up to visit me. He took them out to dinner

and they adored him. He was quite charming and said all of the

things they wanted to hear when it came to taking care of their

daughter.

I remembered the day I got engaged to Ken. I had no idea

what he was planning. He wanted to try a restaurant

downtown that was very fancy and expensive. I knew I had a

A Mother's Influence

dress in my closet that was perfect for a special occasion. He picked me up in his Jaguar and commented on how beautiful I looked.

After we finished dinner, he said, "Anolese, there's something I've have been meaning to ask you."

"What is it, Ken?"

He got down on one knee and asked, "Anolese, will you marry me?"

I hadn't expected to hear those words.

"Ken, I come from a very southern and strict upbringing. I want to say yes. But I need to know that you have talked with my dad and have gotten his permission."

"Yes, of course," Ken said, "I spoke with your dad and he gave me his blessing."

I said, "Then yes, yes, yes, I'll marry you. I'll marry you."

He put a one carat princess cut diamond ring on my finger.

How did he know this was exactly the ring I wanted?

We embraced in the restaurant and shared a long kiss. I was overcome with new emotion - feeling like I was on cloud nine; oblivious to the people in the restaurant who had seen the entire proposal and were clapping. Ken insisted that we celebrate with a bottle of champagne. He had the waiter pour me a full glass of champagne. I took a couple of sips and excused myself. Sobbing, I ran to the restroom. As I stood facing the mirror I cleaned the mascara from around my eyes and looked at the ring on my left finger. I was so excited. I kept saying to myself, *I'm getting married.*

When I returned to the table, I could feel a glow, like I had wings on my feet. My dreams of having a family were coming true. Ken got up to pull out my chair. He made another toast to our lives together he insisted that I finish the glass of champagne to celebrate our lives together.

A Mother's Influence

As we left the restaurant, I felt a little light headed due to drinking a glass of champagne. We were almost home and I was saying to myself, how *did we get here so quickly?*

Ken helped me out of the car like he usually did after a date. I told him that he did not have to come inside.

Ken insisted. He said I seemed a little off balanced and that he wanted to make sure that his bride was going to be okay. As soon as he opened the door, I could feel his lips on mine kissing me good night.

I said, "I love you," and he let himself out.

As I walked down the hall to my room, I began to unzip my dress. A few moments later, it felt like someone was helping me. I imagined a hand on my back unzipping my dress and my bra fell to the floor. Suddenly, Ken turned me around and I felt like putty in his hands. I felt as if I was having an out- of -body experience, as if I was in a trance and what was happening to me was actually happening to someone else. I tried to stop him, but he scooped me up and carried me to the bed. Ken began to take off his shoes and undress himself.

I was so intoxicated with the evening and the engagement that I wondered if this could be real. - *This is so surreal, I thought. I must be dreaming or watching a movie.* - Was I hallucinating? Ken had kissed me goodnight at the door.

I woke up the next morning and couldn't believe I had overslept. I was uncertain of what had happened the night before. I walked to the bathroom and I felt sore; I had an ache in my head. I went back into my bedroom to retrieve some pain pills. When I returned to the bedroom, the phone was ringing. It was Ken. I went to sit down on the side of the bed and I noticed blood on the sheets. I asked Ken what had happened last night.

"We made love," he said.

"What do you mean?" I asked.

A Mother's Influence

"We made love," Ken repeated.

"But you know I'm a virgin and I was saving myself for my wedding night. What did you do to me? I never would have let this happen!"

"But you did," Ken said, and "you enjoyed every bit of it. In fact, you kept asking for more. I had to leave before you wore me out. I had to be fresh for my big meeting today."

I screamed that I hated him for what he had done to me.

"I thought you were kidding." Ken said. "Who saves themselves these days? Who does that? I'll be over later. We'll talk about this then. I need to get back to work."

I told Ken, "There is no later. I don't want you here. You stole my virginity."

"Anolese, calm down. It's not the end of the world! We love each other and we plan to spend the rest of our lives together. We would have made love, eventually."

"That's no excuse for what you did to me," I said.

I was glad when he didn't show up. I called into work and told my manager that I was sick and would be home for a few days. Samantha called later that morning to find out if I had the flu. When I tried to answer her, I started crying. "Anolese, I will be there as soon as I get off from work," she said.

I ripped the sheets from the bed to put on fresh sheets. I saw a condom wrapper on the far side of the bed. It infuriated me even more and I began to cry again. I crawled in the freshly made bed into a fetal position and mourned the loss of my virginity. I knew I had to get up and call my doctor. He was an MD, not a gynecologist, but he delivered babies and he had become my friend. Dr. Horne told me I could come in at one for an examination. I told him exactly what had happened.

After he performed an examination, he confirmed that I was no longer a virgin. There had been sexual intercourse. I told Dr. Horne that I couldn't remember exactly what had happened and that I remembered being light headed. Dr. Horne decided that he would also do some blood work. Dr. Horne made several other recommendations. He also gave me a written excuse for the time off. When I finally stopped crying, he told me that I should talk with a therapist.

I left the doctor's office and went straight home. A few hours later, Samantha arrived at my apartment. I was on the sofa. I think I'd been there for at least three hours in the same spot. I was able to talk to Samantha without crying. I didn't have any tears left. I was just angry. I told her what he'd said happened.

Samantha sat there motionless, not knowing what to say until she blurted out that she was shocked by his behavior. She began to call him all kinds of names. She said, "I can't believe what you're telling me. He painted a totally different picture of himself." She began to question me and said, "Are you sure that's what happened?"

I told her I didn't know what had happened. I couldn't remember.

Samantha said, "If he did this to you, what else is he capable of doing? I'm going to ask Elisa to have her brother, who is a law enforcement officer, do a background check on him. The only thing I'll say to Elisa is that we both love you and your relationship is getting serious and that we need to look out for our friend."

I didn't go to work for several days. Ken would call to check on me, but I didn't want to talk with him. I still loved him, but I felt betrayed. I didn't know what to feel anymore.

My parents called to check on me because I hadn't called home in a few days. I told them that I'd been sick with the flu, but was getting better.

A Mother's Influence

Mama said, "Anolese, do you need for me to come and take care of you?"

I told her no and that I was getting better every day. I told my Mama that I'd call her in a few days. I knew I had to make good on that comment because they worried about me. I went back to work and I was a zombie. I was waiting the two weeks for my next doctor's appointment. Also, Samantha didn't want to pressure Elisa to get the information from her brother, so she waited patiently.

My doctor's appointment was coming up in a few days. I kept Ken at bay every time he called me. I told him that I didn't want to talk with him.

He told me that I was just being silly. He told me that he had to go out of town for a few days and would see me when he got back, whether I wanted him to or not.

I requested a vacation day for my follow-up appointment with Dr. Horne. As I walked into his office, I saw a very puzzling look on his face. Dr. Horne stated that my blood results were back and it showed small traces of rohypnol, which is a date rape drug.

He said, "Anolese, that could explain why you couldn't remember what happened that night. I also need your permission to perform an HIV test."

I started crying and couldn't believe what I was hearing. I thought back to what Ken had said to me, that I was begging for more. I only found one condom. I asked myself, *Could Ken have had unprotected sex with me?* I felt faint, but gave my consent for the test. I was so glad that I'd asked my boss for a vacation day because in my state of mind I never could have gone back to work.

Later that evening, Samantha came over and told me what Elisa's brother had found out. Samantha said, "Brace yourself. He's a dirty, no good, low down... Ken's married and has a wife who's pregnant. Elisa's brother sent one of his fellow officers to Ken's home in Chicago on a rouse after Elisa told him that he was your boyfriend. I'm so sorry to be the one to give you this news."

I collapsed to the floor. I couldn't believe a human being was capable of such deception. I asked myself, *what had I done to deserve this?*

I had a few days to digest the information before Ken came back to town. This time when he called, I didn't tell him he couldn't come by. Instead, I invited him over and I looked forward to seeing him around 8:00 p.m. that evening. I called Samantha and asked her if she would come over and be there with me. I asked her to wait in the laundry room, so she could hear everything that was going on in case we needed to call the police.

Ken rang the doorbell and I let him in. He tried to kiss me. "I am glad you came to your senses, Anolese," he said.

"So tell me why you did what you did?" I said.

He said, "I love you, baby. I slipped you something to make you relax."

"You mean, you drugged me? You took advantage of me. Why?"

"I've never had the privilege of being with a virgin before and I wanted to know how it felt."

"You mean, your wife wasn't a virgin before you got her pregnant?"

He had a look of surprise on his face, he was shocked. Finally, he said, "What do you mean? What are you talking about?"

"I'm just as clever as you, asshole. Get out of my house. I never want to hear from you again or I'll press charges for rape."

"You can't prove I raped you. I'll tell everyone that you wanted it because I had given you a one carat diamond and you considered it my reward. By the way, I never asked your dad for permission to marry you. I love my wife. I just wanted to be your first."

"I can prove it, you asshole. Get out!!!"

"Not before I get my ring back."

"Your ring just became payment for my pain and suffering. You'll never see it again. You got more out of the deal than I did."

That's when Samantha appeared with two phones in her hand; the house phone and her cell phone.

"Ken, I've recorded the entire conversation and all I have to do is press another "1" on the phone and the police will be here," Samantha said. "They've already been put on standby for a possible disturbance at this address."

Ken said a few choice words and finally said, "You keep it. I got what I wanted. You deserve it. Thanks for the experience."

I threw the first thing I saw at his head on his way out the door. The vase was thrown with such force it shattered into small pieces. I told him that if he ever mentioned my name again, I would contact his wife and play the tape for his friends.

He continued to call me a few times and I continued to threaten him. I told him that I would drive to Hyde Park, Chicago and tell his wife personally what a dog he was. My outburst finally ended his phone calls.

I called in for a week's vacation to mentally heal and await the results of the HIV and pregnancy test. I was going to let the results of the test dictate what my next steps would be. I just wanted it all to go away and be erased from my memory. I didn't think that I needed a therapist. I was a strong woman and told myself that I'd get over this. I toiled over what to do.

A Mother's Influence

I'd thought about filing charges against him, but I didn't want my parents to find out, or anyone to know what had happened to me. This secret was going to remain with me and Samantha. At the end of the week, I received a phone call from Dr. Horne and the results of the pregnancy and HIV test were both negative. Dr. Horne suggested that I should be tested again for HIV in six weeks and again in twelve weeks.

I decided not to focus on the testing and put it in the back of my mind. As a distraction, I decided to let my job consume my thoughts by taking on more responsibility.

It had taken two years but now I was a full time employee with Quick Flash and had just been promoted. Samantha wanted to get some lunch later in the cafeteria. I said, "No way." Samantha informed me that Ken had left to take a job as an attorney with another company. I closed my eyes for a moment and said a little prayer; relieved that I would never have to see his face again. I could have ruined his career.

Chapter 3

My hopes, dreams and wishes had fallen apart. I wanted someone in my life. I started to ask myself if it was just because I was lonely. After being personally and physically violated, I never felt safe again. I wanted someone around me so that I could feel safe and get a good night sleep. I know that was no reason to jump from the fire into the frying pan.

I decided that the best thing for me to do was to continue to live my life and just focus on my career at Quick Flash. My focus was going to be on me and my well - being from this point on. I had been going to Design Baptist Church, but I became paranoid because I felt like everyone was looking at me and that the minister's sermons were directed at me every Sunday. I decided to visit other churches. I finally found a church that I felt comfortable in. I enjoyed the service so much

A Mother's Influence

that I found myself there every Sunday, so I joined the

congregation and eventually moved my membership.

I had begun to attend Sunday school which was an hour

before the service. After attending the First Baptist Church for

several weeks, the congregation was planning for revival

services and I was on the hospitality committee. We had

invited a different church for each of the five nights of revival

services.

Our guest for the Monday night service was the Salem Baptist

Church. While standing at the door greeting the guests, a

woman introduced herself to me as Mary Summers. I said,

"Good evening, my name is Anolese. Is this your first visit to

our church?

She said, "Yes."

I said, "Well I hope you enjoy the service."

She seemed nice. She was conservatively dressed and she was very talkative. It was almost time for the minister to begin preaching when I walked into the church and noticed a seat beside the lady who had introduced herself to me earlier. I sat down next to her and she smiled. When the service ended, Mary looked at me and said, "Will you be here tomorrow night?"

I said, "Yes."

Mary came to the revival service every night for five nights. She came in early just to talk and tell me how much she was enjoying the services. I often sat next to her during the services. The last night of revival service, Mary asked me, "Would you like to visit my church some Sunday?"

I told her that I would love to but didn't know when that would be possible because most Sundays I taught Sunday school as a backup teacher.

Mary said, "Anolese, maybe we can meet for lunch?"

A Mother's Influence

We exchanged information and I really didn't expect to hear from her as quickly as I did. She called two days later and invited me out to lunch. She told me that she enjoyed my energy, my warm smile and my sense of fashion. I was rather puzzled by her comment, but I met her for lunch at the Mountain View Family Diner.

Mary was at least twenty five years older than me. I thought that maybe I was the daughter that she'd never had. I asked about her family.

Mary said, "I have two children, a twenty year older daughter and a thirty two year old son. I have a great family and I love my children very much. I guess I just needed a little time to myself. So thank you for having lunch with me."

I was still skeptical about our lunch date. Mary talked about her children during most of our lunch hour. I was able to get a few comments in. Mary picked up the check for lunch so being the person I am, I said, "We should do this again."

Mary immediately said, "Let's meet again two weeks from today."

I agreed.

I called my girlfriend, Samantha, to tell her about the weirdness of the outing. Samantha told me to cancel the next lunch meeting. Samantha said, "Mary seems like she has some ulterior motive."

I told Samantha that I was smart enough to figure that out, I just wanted to know what it was.

As I sat at my desk during the week my mind wondered why Mary had befriended me and what she could possibly want from our encounters. I wasn't ready to call it a relationship or friendship. We'd just met. A week and a half had almost come and gone and I thought about cancelling my lunch date with Mary, but I was curious.

A Mother's Influence

Mary was already at the restaurant when I got there and had been seated. As usual, she did most of the talking. She talked about her daughter, Mia, who was in college and she kept saying Mia needed a summer job. When I didn't comment, Mary said, "Anolese, does your company employ kids for the summer?"

I told her they did but mainly the children of their employees. Sometimes, Quick Flash would hire other kids. I encouraged Mary to have Mia apply, just to see if she could get in for the twelve - week summer program.

Mary finally started to ask me questions about myself. "Anolese, tell me a little bit about yourself? Were you born and raised in the Buffalo area?"

I said "No. I'm originally from a little town in Georgia."

Mary asked, "How long have you lived in Buffalo? Where did you go to school? How often do you go home to visit? Are you parents still living? Have you ever been married? Do you have a boyfriend?"

I tried to keep up with her questions, but I felt as if I was being interrogated.

I thanked Mary for meeting me for lunch. "Anolese, lunch was great." Mary said, "I'd like for you to come over for dinner Sunday to meet the rest of my family. I have been telling them about you."

I said to myself, *telling them what?* I wanted to decline her offer but reluctantly, I accepted. I was just getting in deeper and deeper.

I had Samantha over that evening after lunch with Mary. I told Samantha about the series of questions Mary had asked me. I told Samantha about the invitation for Sunday dinner.

Samantha said, "You might as well go with the flow and see what she has up her sleeve."

A Mother's Influence

I attended church on Sunday and the minister's sermon was about being aware of wolves in sheep's clothing. It was a great sermon and it got me thinking about Mary and her possible ulterior motive. I got to her house around four o'clock that afternoon. Mary greeted me at the door, as I walked in - I loved the way she'd decorated her house. It was my style and it looked as if we both shopped at HomeGoods, Marshalls, and TJ Maxx. We finally had something in common. I had begun to relax in an environment that I was familiar with. Mary summoned the rest of her family to the living room. She introduced them to me. She had talked about Mia and I was anxious to meet her. Mia was very reserved and didn't say much. I met her husband John. Mary told me that John was a deacon at their church. When I shook his hand and felt the calluses, I assumed that he must have a job working with his hands. After shaking John's hand, he motioned for me to have a seat on the sofa. I quickly scanned the room. As I looked over to the book case, there were several shelves dedicated to the history of religious beliefs. I asked myself, *does that have anything to do with my suspicions about Mary?*

Mary mentioned that her son was also coming for dinner. Mary said that she'd told him about me and that he was anxious to meet me.

I asked myself, *is she trying to fix me up with her son? Is that what she's up to?*

A few minutes later, I heard someone at her door. A tall muscular man walked in and Mary immediately said, "Anolese, this is my son, Adrian."

Adrian had a nice smile. "Hello Anolese, he said." "Mother talks about you often. I feel as if I know you already."

Mary immediately said, "Dinner is ready. You two can get acquainted after dinner."

A Mother's Influence

John, Mary's husband, said the longest grace I have every heard over a meal. He thanked God for everything. When John finished the prayer, the food was no longer hot. I tried not to show any facial expressions because I needed as many prayers and blessings as I could get at this point in my life. However, I realized that John didn't know the difference between blessing the food and praying. The table conversation was centered on me and I wasn't comfortable talking about myself. I felt like I was being interrogated again by each family member.

Adrian was very attentive and he catered to me. In spite of the unusual circumstances, I started to enjoy his company. I decided that all men couldn't be dogs, but at this point in my life I had very little proof. *Am I losing my mind? It's too soon*, I told myself, *to think about being with another man.* I realized my life had changed. The person that I'd become since moving to Buffalo, NY was not the same girl who'd moved from Georgia. I didn't even recognize myself anymore.

Mary called me two weeks after our Sunday dinner and told me that Mia had gotten an interview for the summer job at Quick Flash and they had offered her the job. I told Mary that was great. I later found out that Mia had been hired into one of the units I supported.

I found myself going to Mary's house every other Sunday after church and seeing Adrian there. It was nice getting to know him and his family. Mary did more talking than anyone else. Even though I liked the southern food she prepared, I felt like it was an extension of church. Religion was the only conversation in that house. I couldn't take it anymore, so I began to decline her offers most Sundays. I thought of myself as more spiritual than religious.

A month later, Adrian called and asked me out for coffee. I declined, but he persisted. I felt it was innocent enough. He had told me that he was single and had never been married.

A Mother's Influence

Maybe he just wants a friend? He also told me that he sang in the male choir at his church.

I tried to take it slow, but I was truly smitten by him. We went out every weekend for eight months. Adrian wasn't very romantic. I often wondered why he never tried to go any further than a kiss. I had a great time with him and I was also glad that not having sex wasn't an issue, which would have probably complicated my life. I had convinced myself that life was starting to look up. We went to dinner almost every Friday night. He was into fish frys. That had never been the norm for my family growing up in Georgia. It was always hamburgers or pizza on Friday nights.

Most of our dates centered on church functions because he wanted to be around his mother. He was a real mama's boy. One day, Adrian asked me if I would go on a weekend trip with him.

"I'll have to think about it," I said.

He immediately said, "Anolese, I'll pay for us to sleep in separate rooms."

After that comment, I agreed. He wanted to go to Niagara Falls, Canada. I was excited.

When we arrived in Niagara Falls, it was raining. We checked into our separate rooms and then left the hotel to take in the sites. We walked around half the day in the rain. We went on a bus tour and visited a flower garden. As we stepped on the bus and sat behind an elderly couple, they asked us, "How long have you two been married?"

We just looked at each other and smiled. I think that was the first time I realized that I had strong feelings for him.

Later that evening, Adrian said to me, "Wear something nice."

I asked him, "Where are were going?"

A Mother's Influence

He said, "I'm taking you somewhere special. It's a surprise."

I didn't know where we were going until we pulled up in front of a church. He said, "My church is having a conference here and I thought this would be a nice place to bring you, so you can meet some of the people from my congregation."

I tried not to show the disappointment I was feeling.

After the church conference, he took me out to dinner. We were having an okay time. We talked about what we were looking for in a mate and just life in general. Adrian said, "When you get married, Anolese, how many children do you want?"

I told Adrian that I knew I wanted children but I had never really thought about how many. I wondered where he was going with the conversation. I was hoping that he wasn't getting any ideas because I wasn't ready to make any commitments to anyone at this point in my life.

I tuned out for a few minutes and began to recall the conversation that I had with Samantha a few weeks ago when I had introduced him to Samantha. She didn't like him. She said there was something about him that she couldn't put her finger on. Samantha said, "Adrian seems like he's over the top around his religious beliefs." She told me that when I had left her alone with him, he seemed as if he had a controlling personality. "Anolese, I just can't put my finger on it, but there's something that bothers me about him. Be careful. I don't think he's the one."

I didn't know if Adrian was asking me any questions because I hadn't been listening to him. The last thing I heard him say was, "Baby, are you ready to go?" I didn't answer him because I was still gathering my thoughts. He paid for dinner and we left the restaurant.

As we approached the car, Adrian's tone of voice became serious and I began to focus on what he was saying. He told me that the reason he had never gotten married was because he wanted a "wholesome girl" and he was never able to find one - until now.

I said to myself, *Wholesome?* *"What does he mean by that?"* He had never tried to do anything but kiss me. But in my heart, I knew what he meant. In my mind, I said, *you don't know me.*

Adrian said that he had been saving himself for his wedding night. He told me that he'd been tempted many times, but sex was the devil's way of interfering with God's work. Adrian went on to say, "My mom told me that you're a wholesome church girl and you've never been married, so I know you're a virgin." Adrian was making a statement more than he was asking a question. We were pulling up to the hotel when he made his comment.

The valet was opening my door and I got out of the car. Adrian came around to meet me and we walked into the hotel together. I told Adrian I was extremely tired. He kissed me on the forehead and said, "Good night." I couldn't wait to get back to my hotel room and process what Adrian and I had talked about.

I decided to phone my best friend. Samantha answered on the first ring. She said, "Anolese, I was hoping you'd call. How is your romantic weekend going? Tell me what's happened so far. I need details, girl."

"Samantha, I didn't know what to expect with Adrian this weekend, but I didn't expect that the highlight of our trip was a church conference."

Samantha immediately said, "You've got to be kidding me."

I said, "I wish I wasn't. It was two hours of him introducing me to his congregation."

A Mother's Influence

Samantha asked, "Doesn't he know that Niagara Falls is for lovers?"

"Well," I said, "at least we had dinner afterwards. When we got to the restaurant, the waiter came to take our order and he proceeded to order chicken for both of us. I said, Adrian, I think I want flounder tonight, and he said, "You'll enjoy the chicken". I sort of wanted to banter back and forth but I chose not to in front of the waiter. When the waiter left, I said, what was that about? Adrian said, I've known you for almost a year so I think I know what you like to eat. I was so angry with him, I just picked at my food."

"Anolese, I'm speechless," Samantha said, "what else happened?"

I told her, "Adrian started saying things like, Anolese, how many children do you want? He asked all sorts of questions and I pretty much ignored him. I just moved my food around the plate and couldn't wait to leave the restaurant. I'm sure he must have known I was upset. We finally finished dinner and left the restaurant. As we pulled up to the hotel, the valet opened my door and I got out of the car. Adrian walked around to my door and escorted me into the hotel. I looked at him and told him that I was exhausted and was going to bed. He walked me to my hotel room and kissed me goodnight. Samantha, I'm really tired. Let's talk tomorrow when I get home. I'll call you."

When I woke up around eight thirty the next morning, I knew we were checking out at around eleven. I didn't wait for Adrian to call me. I decided to order coffee and a bagel from room service. Adrian called around ten o'clock and asked me how long it would take me to get ready. I told him I was packed and ready. Adrian told me Carlton, one of the church members, had called him and asked if he could ride back to Buffalo with us. I said, "I don't mind." However, I don't think Adrian was asking me. I just put in my two cents anyway.

A Mother's Influence

Adrian told me that he'd be at my door in twenty minutes. I said, "Why don't I meet you in the hotel lobby." He agreed.

Adrian and I met in the lobby. He took my overnight bag and put it in the trunk. We got in the car and drove to another hotel to pick up Carlton. Carlton greeted us and went to get into the back seat when Adrian said, "Anolese, you might be more comfortable in the back seat." I got out of the car and got into the back seat. It was perfectly okay with me because I didn't want to converse with either of them. I couldn't wait to get home and get out of the car.

Adrian took me home first and he walked up to the door with my bags. He kissed me on the cheek and told me he had a great time and would call me later. I'm sure that I looked at him with disgust. I really didn't care if I ever saw him again. I took a nap and when I woke up, I called Samantha to catch her up on the remaining events of the trip.

All she had to say was, "Anolese, he's not the one."

Adrian called me later that evening and said to me, "Do you remember the elderly couple on the tour bus and what they asked us?"

I said, "Of course I do. We should have told them that we weren't married."

Adrian said, "I think we should get married. I know this is the first time that I'm saying it," but I love you. "How do you feel about me?"

I told Adrian that I wasn't ready to make a life time commitment to anyone. While I told myself, *I never should have gone on that trip to Niagara Falls with him.*

When he hung up the phone, I'm sure he was puzzled. I'm sure I seemed aloof. He wanted a virgin and that day had come and gone for me. I knew that I needed space from him. From that point on, I was non-committal when he called and asked me out. Each time, I'd come up with a different excuse. I slowly backed away from him. I wasn't the wholesome young lady he was looking for. I no longer wore the label he desired.

I had made up so many excuses for my behavior that I had a hard time keeping up with what I was saying to him when he called.

I decided to stop avoiding him and invite him over because I had been ignoring him and not returning his phone calls. I had actually been ignoring his entire family. Mary continued to ask me over for dinner and I would always decline. Mary asked me if something was wrong; if she had done something to offend me. I immediately said, "No." I told her that work had been consuming all of my free time.

When Adrian arrived, I told him that he'd made some assumptions about me and that I wasn't who he thought I was. I'd been anticipating his question to me and wasn't quite sure how I would answer him. I wasn't ready to reveal my entire secret. *How do you tell someone that you were raped?*

Violated? I didn't think he would understand and I'm sure no matter what the circumstances were he would have a problem with me not being a virgin. *Have I come across the only other man in the world who hasn't fooled around?* I was falling for him and I probably could have pulled it off. *But how could I live with myself if I lie to him?* Lying was not an option.

Adrian finally asked the question that I was dreading.

He asked, "Anolese, are you a virgin?"

I said, "No." I could not bring myself to elaborate.

"You're right, I did assume you were a virgin." Adrian said, "I can't believe my mother introduced you to me."

I told him that he should not have depended on his mother. He should have found out for himself what he wanted to know and, if he'd asked me months ago, I would have told him. I abruptly said, "Since you don't want damaged goods, I

A Mother's Influence

think its best that we don't see each other anymore. In fact, you should leave."

I never heard from Adrian or his mother again. It was as if I told them that I had leprosy.

Two weeks later, as I was preparing for a meeting, Peter, one of the supervisors walked into my office and told me that he needed to talk to me about one of the summer students. Peter told me that there was a female who was very disruptive. What he noticed was the female would change into very provocative attire, which could be seen through her thin white uniform. It was apparent that she didn't wear a bra and the outline of her nipples showed very clearly. Her attire had become a safety hazard because she had the men falling over pallets and the injury rate had doubled since she took the job. Peter stated, "I have talked with her and she continues to parade around. I would like to terminate her."

I told Peter that I needed to see all of the documentation. When I received the paperwork, I was shocked to learn that it was Mia Summers, Adrian's sister. After reading the warnings that Peter had documented, and seeing how many conversations they'd had with no change in Mia's attire or behavior, I agreed that Mia should be terminated.

Peter asked me if I would assist him with the termination. He told me that he felt uncomfortable terminating her without a witness. He shared with me that there were other rumors of sexual inappropriateness in the workplace that he was unable to confirm. I agreed to be in the room when he terminated her.

Peter went to get her. I was not looking forward to this encounter, as I was shocked to know that she was exhibiting such behaviors given what I knew about her family. The thought crossed my mind that I should have another HR person

A Mother's Influence

be involved with the termination, but no one else was
available, and after all, this was my job.

Mia followed Peter into my office. She was shocked to
see me. Peter said, "Mia, this is Anolese Turner, our human
resource manager."

Mia never made eye contact. I assumed she was
embarrassed; I would have been in that situation. Peter told
her that due to the fact that he had written her up several times
regarding her inappropriate attire and there had been no change
in her behavior, she was being terminated. "Your behavior
will no longer be tolerated."

Mia said, "Fine, I didn't like working with all these stuck
up people anyway."

Peter gave her a termination letter and I had a female
group leader escort her back to clean out her locker. When she
returned with a few personal items, I escorted her off the
premises. At that point, she asked me not to tell her mother. I

told her that I'd follow the company policy and not tell anyone. As she left, I told her that I was disappointed in her behavior, especially since I knew her parents.

Mia looked back at me and said, "I thought you would be on my side since my brother told me that you're not even a virgin."

I was shocked to hear those words. *Why would Adrian have told his sister?* This just reinforced that I should have left the asshole sooner. *Apparently, that's why his mother never calls me anymore.*

I thought it would take a long time to get over Adrian, but I realized that I was not as committed in the relationship as I'd thought. I wanted him to be this caring person and to love me for me. Adrian had wanted what I wanted a few years ago. The difference was I - was looking for my soul mate not another virgin.

A Mother's Influence

Adrian made it perfectly clear what he wanted and I did not meet his criteria. He didn't even try to understand the circumstances. It made me question my judgment in people. He was so heavily involved in the church that I thought he would have practiced what he preached. *Is it written somewhere that a man has to marry a virgin? Should I have told him what had happened to me?* I told myself that it probably wouldn't have mattered. However, when I told him that I was not a virgin, he didn't even ask anymore questions. As I reflected back on the relationship, he never really stopped to get to know me.

I thought if I found a guy that was in the church he would not judge me. I told myself that not everyone who attends church is Christ- like. *Okay,* I said to myself, *I did the right thing.*

When I told Samantha that Adrian and I had broken up, she said, "Too bad, but I'm glad you found out now. I never did like the super religious types. He was too conceited and was full of himself."

We both laughed.

Chapter 4

It had been three months and the last thing I wanted to do was deal with another man in my life. I started to redecorate my house and decided to begin with the bedroom. I contacted a painting company and they told me they would send over one of their best painters.

In preparation for the painter, I bribed a few of my friends with pizza and wings to help me move all of the furniture out of the room. We left the bed and covered it up. A day later, the painter showed up. He introduced himself as Joseph. As I stood facing the painter on the ladder, I glanced up and couldn't miss his hazel eyes and the contrast of his mocha skin. I had to walk behind him because he awakened a lust in me that I didn't want him to detect. While behind him, I looked up at the paint color and I loved the concoction that I'd had come up with. I also noticed his physique and was even more turned on. I decided that I should leave the room while I could still walk.

The last man I was this turned on by was Ryan and that was a long time ago. As I returned to the bedroom to ask Joseph if he wanted anything to drink, I couldn't speak because I noticed that he was no longer wearing a shirt. All I noticed was his six-pack and the sweat dripping off his mocha skin. I immediately asked, "Is it too hot in here?"

He said, "No, I got paint on my shirt." I asked if he wanted me to wash it for him before the paint dried and he said, "If you don't mind."

"Where is your shirt?" I asked.

When reaching for his shirt, I brushed up against his naked chest; we stared at each other for a moment and then he kissed me. For a quick second, I thought about retreating. Instead, I gave in to the lust I was feeling. One thing led to another and we found ourselves in bed. I rolled away from him and started to question myself. *Who the hell are you?*

What are you doing? I've never done this before. I'd just met

this man. *What's happening to me?* I was embarrassed by the

fact that having sex felt so good. I didn't want to confuse this

with making love because I didn't know anything about this

man. But I wanted to get to know him better. *You know*

better, I kept saying to myself. I didn't love him, but I enjoyed

it and wanted to do it again. I didn't care if I ever got my

bedroom painted, as long as I could continue to feel this way.

Being in Joseph's arms made me lose touch with reality.

I was falling in lust. I wasn't looking for substance. I

was just looking to be with a man to fulfill my dreams and the

void that others had left in my life. Joseph left that day without

finishing the paint job. He promised to be back and finish

within the next two days. Joseph called me that evening and

we talked for hours. He made me feel so comfortable. We

talked about our lives and our work and he told me that both

his parents were deceased - that he and his siblings were raised by his Aunt Kim, his mother's sister. I immediately felt sad that Joseph didn't have the loving parents that I'd had growing up. Joseph said that he'd been in Vietnam for two tours of duty. I told him how proud I was of our servicemen who were giving their lives for our freedom.

Joseph asked, "Anolese, where do you work and what do you do when you are not at work?"

"I work at Quick Flash in Human Resources I love to decorate and find old things and make them new again," I replied.

When we finally got off the phone, I was able to get a few hours of sleep before going to work. I must have lain awake for hours thinking about how happy I was that I'd finally found someone who wasn't judging me. I did question my behavior around sleeping with someone I'd just met. I had never done that before. I'd wanted my first time making love to be with someone special and someone who truly loved me.

A Mother's Influence

Joseph returned to finish the paint job the next day. He worked diligently with very little conversation until he was completely finished. He offered to help me put the room back together. Afterwards, when the room looked perfect, he invited me out to dinner. I think we were both a little exhausted and I really didn't feel like preparing a meal, so I took him up on his offer.

At dinner, we continued to get to know each other and talk about our lives. He told me that he had a full time job at a small printing company and that's why it took him more than a day to finish painting my bedroom. "Painting is a side job for me," Joseph said, "It relaxes me and frees my mind from the day-to-day bouts of anxiety."

Joseph and I spent lots of time together, but most of it was making love. I was beginning to feel as if someone genuinely cared for me. However, something in the back of my mind was causing me to take a deeper look at how I was raised in respect to being married before having sex. I raised those concerns with Joseph about being intimate in a relationship with a man before marriage. He agreed with me and said that we should sustain from sex and just get to really know each other. Most of the things we did together just involved the two of us. We were in our own little world. Joseph and I went on several dates; picnics in the park, outdoor concerts, movies and out to dinner. I never really met that many of his friends. I met a few of the guys he worked with. Joseph was mainly a loner. "People always let you down," he said. I figured being in the service had something to do with that.

He had told me that he didn't like to be around a lot of people. "Anolese, I don't want to share you with the whole world. I'm selfish. I want you just for me."

I thought that was sweet. It felt good to be needed. What I didn't realize was that I was being isolated from my friends and family. After several weeks, he eventually introduced me to his brothers and sisters. They were all raised by his Aunt Kim. I introduced Joseph to my siblings in Buffalo. They didn't seem to like him as much as I did, but I didn't care. He was the one I'd chosen.

Several weeks later, Joseph stopped over one night and wanted to talk. I told him it was late and that I needed to get some sleep because I had to give a presentation the next morning.

Joseph said, "Anolese, I think we should get married. I love you. Let's just elope."

I told Joseph that I loved him, as well, but eloping was out of the question.

Joseph said, "Let's just have a small wedding and invite a few friends."

I agreed and gave into his wishes for a small wedding; one that we could pull off within a few months.

I called my parents and told them that Joseph had asked me to marry him. My father said, "How can he ask you to marry him when he hasn't asked me?" I told my dad that was old fashioned.

Mama said, "So when are we going to meet this guy who has bad manners?"

I knew my parents would have a problem with Joseph disrespecting them without asking for my hand in marriage, but they agreed.

When we went to Georgia so my parents could meet Joseph, he turned up the volume on his charm. They loved what they heard and saw. On the other hand, my siblings weren't very impressed with him. They kept saying that there was something about him that didn't feel right. Every chance they got, they questioned me about him.

A Mother's Influence

Joseph was only telling me the things he wanted me to know - like a typical man. My questions to him were not specific enough. Therefore, I was unable to answer my sibling's questions to their satisfaction.

The next few weeks of my life were spent preparing for my wedding day and helping Joseph find us a place to live. I spent hours packing and getting ready for the move and our new life together.

The day of my wedding, I was standing outside the church on the sidewalk waiting to walk down the aisle. A female was passing by and asked, "Are you marrying Joseph?" I didn't answer her and she added, "I guess he painted your bedroom, too."

I didn't know what to say or how to feel, but something in my gut told me to get in my car and drive away. I had no idea of what was to come and I began to rationalize whether or not I should marry him.

My entire family was in the church waiting for me to walk down the aisle. I knew they were not too keen on me marrying Joseph due to a short courtship, or maybe it was deeper than that, but I didn't want to let anyone down. I had no idea that at that moment, I was doing more harm to myself than anyone else could.

I finally entered the church and, as my father handed me off to Joseph, I saw a look in Joseph's eyes that I'd never seen before. And I was suddenly afraid. The look made me feel as if I'd become his purchased possession.

From the look Joseph had given me, I was distracted by fear. All I heard of the wedding vows was my promise to obey. We took a few pictures, left the church and headed for the reception. One of my bridesmaids came up to me and said, "Anolese, you look tense. Take a few sips of my margarita." I did and it calmed my nerves.

A Mother's Influence

From the decorations to the cake to our first dance as husband and wife, the reception was perfect. While dancing with my father, I wanted to hold on and never let go. He had been an unfailing hero. Now, I was stepping into the world of the unknown. The reception was winding down and Joseph and I were preparing to leave. We said our good nights and left for our first night as husband and wife. Joseph had made reservation at the Ritz Carlton in the bridal suite. We had a magical night together.

The next day, we started out on our honeymoon. I had forgotten all about the previous doubts before the wedding. It was a distant memory in the back of my mind. We were driving to New Orleans. On the way there, we'd planned to stop and see Kim, the aunt who'd raised him, because she was sick and unable to attend our wedding.

When we got to Biloxi, Mississippi, Joseph got me settled in at his aunt's home and said that he was going out to pick up a few things and wouldn't be long. But he never came back. I slept alone that night. When he returned the next day, he was drunk. His clothes stunk of alcohol, stale marijuana and perfume. At that moment, it hit me and I started to question myself. *Who is this person that I just pledged my love to for the rest of my life?* I swallowed the panic back down in my throat. I could tell that he'd been smoking marijuana. He went directly to the kitchen and came back with a platter full of food. It was enough for him and several others. I then realized that I didn't know him at all. I was afraid to question him about where he'd been all night because of his demeanor. I went in to the kitchen to get away from him when his aunt said, "Anolese, you seem like an intelligent girl. I can't believe you married Joseph. He's no good. Being in Vietnam messed him up and he's never been the same."

I replied, "Why would you say that about him? He's been nothing but kind and supportive, and he loves you. He sends you money all the time."

A Mother's Influence

Kim said, "That's not love. It's obligation."

I walked away from her.

When Joseph woke up after sleeping most of the day, I told him what Kim had said. I knew after the words came out of my mouth that I never should have spoken them. I could see a rage in his eyes.

"Start packing," Joseph told me. "We're leaving in a couple of hours."

I said, "Joseph, I thought we were going to be here a few days, so I could do some sight seeing and some shopping?"

He looked at me and said, "Pack," and he walked away.

A few minutes later, I could hear him arguing with Kim and he stormed through the house and took our luggage to the car.

"Joseph, I'm going to tell Kim goodbye."

Joseph said, "Anolese, get in the car!"

I didn't recognize this man that I was calling my husband. I knew it would be about a two hour drive to New Orleans. I didn't know what to say to him. I didn't want to get him angry but I had a few questions I wanted answered. I knew I had to watch my tone with him but I finally said to Joseph, "Do you love me? Why did you marry me?"

Joseph said, "Why not? If I married you, you're mine and you have to perform whenever I need you to. I married you for sex. Just shut up! I don't want to talk to you any more, so turn the radio on. I don't know why you're asking me these stupid questions. You came on to me the first day I met you, remember?"

That day was the first of many disappointing days with Joseph. When we reached New Orleans, I was extremely tired and frazzled. I didn't know what to expect. I was a long way from home. I was constantly asking myself what I'd gotten into. It was a honeymoon I would have never wished on my worst enemy. The passion we had before marriage was gone. I was just performing a task, a wifely duty. I just wanted to go home. All Joseph wanted to do was have rough sex with me. *Where did the tenderness go?* I would get up and take a shower.

"Don't use all of the hot water," he'd say - I think he was alluding to the fact that I just tried to wash my skin clean from the filthiness that I felt from being with him. He would always take a nap afterwards. After his nap, he would get up, take a quick shower and put on the cologne that I'd bought him. He would then get dressed for a night out on the town, leaving the hotel without me, not even saying "Goodbye" or "I'll be back soon." This ritual went on every night for the five nights we were in New Orleans. He slept most days and I was not allowed to leave the room. One day, I sneaked out of the room and went to the hotel lobby to purchase a few books and would just read every day. Joseph would say to me, "All

you ever do is read. Where did you get those books?" I
convinced him that I'd brought the books with me. I had
nothing else to do. When he came back to the hotel at two or
three in the early morning, he would reek of stale cigarettes,
booze and perfume. I couldn't wait for this torment to be over.

The drive back to Buffalo was stressful. He never
wanted to stop for anything but gas or snacks. He had
cancelled all of the hotel arrangements and the sightseeing
plans we had on the ride back. The only conversations we had
on the ride back home were of what he expected from me as a
wife. Joseph said, "I don't want any of your girlfriends to
come to the house when I'm not home."

I asked him, "Why?"

Joseph said, "They'll just fill your head full of crap."

I told Joseph that I had very little control over whether
or not they just stopped by. Joseph said, "You need
to find a way to make it happen, or you will suffer!"

A Mother's Influence

When we got back home, he became demanding and treated me more like his property than his wife.

When we got back from our honeymoon, I was told to unpack all of our belongings and make the apartment look decent. I worked well into the night to get everything organized to Joseph's satisfaction. I went to bed around 2:00 a.m. the next morning. As I crawled in bed, Joseph woke up and told me that he was glad that we were married and that I was his wife. He said he was sorry about his behavior and that, he'd try to be better. He kissed me goodnight.

I decided to put the horrible memories associated with our honeymoon behind me. The next day, I pulled out a cookbook that we'd received as a wedding gift and went about looking for something special to make my man for dinner. I had set the table with candles and the china that we'd picked out together. I couldn't wait to see his reaction on how special I'd set the table. I heard the door open. Joseph came in and never spoke to me. He never commented on the hard work that went into making the dinner special. As he sat down, I asked him if he wanted to bless the meal.

Joseph said, "Let's just eat, damn it! I'm hungry." Joseph picked up a bowl on the table and asked, "What is this shit? Where is my normal food? Who told you to prepare some fancy shit? Where is the fried chicken? I don't want this shit." He threw the bowl at me.

I picked up the lamb off the floor and while wiping the sauce from my face and blouse, I started to cry.

"Quit that crying, bitch. Take your ass up stairs and clean yourself up, or I'll give you something to cry about." While I was walking away, he grabbed my arm and pulled me toward him and said, "I didn't mean to do that, but you provoked me. I'm just a simple guy used to eating the same thing. I'm not into this fancy stuff." He began to cry and said,

"Anolese, I'm so sorry. I appreciate what you tried to do and I will never hurt you again."

Afterwards, Joseph said that he was leaving to go to get some fresh air and food. He stated that he was really sorry and would be back soon. Joseph didn't return for several hours. I was in bed, but not asleep. I was just lying there with my eyes closed. Before I could see him, I could smell him when he entered the room. Joseph got in bed, shook me and told me to wake up.

"What's wrong?" I said.

"Take your clothes off, bitch," he said and grabbed the hair on my head, pulled me toward his penis. "It's time to take care of daddy."

I said, "Joseph, stop. You're hurting me. You've been drinking."

He still pushed my head toward his penis but released my hair. After a few minutes of torture, he told me to get on the bed and roll over. It was the most painful sex I'd ever had. I think he thought that he was in my vagina but he wasn't and the pain was excruciating. I couldn't wait for it to be over and for him to fall asleep.

I wanted to call my dad and tell him how Joseph was treating me, but I couldn't. I knew how my father would react. My parents had been married for over thirty years and I'd never seen my father raise his hand to my mother. I had to keep what was going on in our marriage a secret. Joseph had turned on me and I was becoming a statistic, a battered woman.

Why did I allow myself to be blinded by the person he is and what he's becoming everyday? At the same time, I had to decide what my next steps would be. I knew that there was no way I could continue to live with this man. My life consisted of living a lie. I just went to work, cleaned the house and made sure that his food was hot and on the table by seven

o'clock each night. If I had an office party or any type of

event, I would have to make up an excuse to get out of it

because I knew Joseph would be mad and I would suffer the

wrath of his fist. We had good times and bad times together.

For me, the bad far outweighed the good.

Joseph wanted me to get pregnant right away. I saw

this as another form of control. He wanted me to go off the

pill. Of course, I told him I would, but I knew I wasn't going

to. I hated him. Sometimes, I was annoyed at myself for

being in this predicament and I knew things had to change.

After a few months, Joseph wanted to go with me to

my next doctor's visit so we could have a discussion with the

doctor to find out why I was not getting pregnant. I called Dr.

Horne and explained the situation. I told Dr. Horne that I was

trying to find a way out of my abusive relationship with my

husband.

Dr. Horne asked, "Did you marry the same guy that raped you?"

I said, "No."

Dr. Horne finally agreed that he would tell Joseph he'd been running tests on me and, in his opinion, I would probably never be able to conceive a child due to a condition called endometriosis.

After we visited the doctor, the abuse got worse. Joseph was becoming more and more violent and he had a shorter and shorter fuse. Sometimes, he would just punch me for no reason. I realized that lust was not a good reason to get married and we didn't love each other. We tolerated one another.

Joseph led me to believe that he was somebody he really wasn't. I'd thought we were evenly yoked and life was going to be good, even though we had made love before marriage. It had become apparent that he'd been putting on an act of enormous proportions. I don't think he believed in God, nor had any values. I'd been duped again.

I had only been married seven months and I was already planning my exit. I contacted a lawyer. The lawyer asked me if I had made any police reports of the abuse.

I said, "No."

He said in order to help me get out of the marriage, I needed to call the police during or after the abuse. I started keeping a diary of all the things Joseph did or said to me. If he pulled my hair, I mailed it to the lawyer's office. If he hit me, I made sure I took a picture of the bruise.

One day, Joseph said to me, "You're just a dumb bitch that brings home a paycheck." In fact, he asked me if I had deposited money in his account and if I knew the consequences for disobeying him.

I mumbled, "Yes." I knew I was at my breaking point. Getting out of this marriage consumed my thoughts both day and night.

I went over to my neighbor Kathy's apartment to tell her what was going on in my life and what my plans were. I told her I was going to do something to provoke Joseph and she should call the police in case I couldn't get to a phone. She was more than happy to help me because she disliked him.

Kathy said, "Anolese, you are such a nice person. You're always so nice to me and my kids. Thanks again for all the gifts you have given them when you didn't have to."

Kathy also said, "Our walls are paper thin between our apartments and I've overheard a few of your arguments. I realize what a jerk he is. He was saying very hurtful things that I knew weren't true. I could hear him belittling you and calling you stupid. I could almost feel your pain because I've also gone through verbal and physical abuse. That's why I left my husband and moved into this apartment. When I heard the two of you arguing, I felt as though I was reliving the same thing that had happened to me a year ago. But I endured it much longer than you." Kathy was almost in tears when she said, "I'm so glad that you're standing up for yourself."

As I was listening to Kathy talk, my mind went back to that particular day replaying the entire conversation in my head. Joseph was calling me stupid and telling me all the things that I couldn't and wasn't doing right. Joseph ended that conversation by saying, "The only thing you're good for is oral sex and you can't even do that right. A baby knows how to suck a bottle."

When I looked up at Kathy again, I was ashamed. I knew she must have heard the entire conversation, not just the little bit that she shared with me.

I had finally made two police reports and was ready to leave him. I waited until he went to work and packed my car with a few of my belongings and fled to a friend's house. I filed for a divorce the next day.

As I was leaving my friend's house to go to work, Joseph walked up on my blind side and knocked me to the ground. "You bitch" he said, "How dare you think you can leave me? You'll never amount to anything. No one else wants your stupid ass." He left me on the ground hurting, berated, belittled and terrified that he would come back and do it again.

I finally told my sister what was going on. She was never able to keep a secret and immediately told my parents and my brother. My mama had to stop my father from doing something irrational. He was ready to catch a plane to Buffalo and handle Joseph, whatever that meant.

My brother told me he'd paid Joseph a visit to give him a taste of his own medicine. He said he went to my apartment and banged on the door. As soon as Joseph opened the door,

A Mother's Influence

he hit him so hard that he fell backwards. My brother said to

Joseph, "I wanted you to know how it felt when you knocked

my sister to the ground. I've never liked you and I've always

wanted to kick your ass. I've always known you weren't the

man for my sister, when I saw you cuddled up with another

woman at a nightclub two months after you were married. I

tolerated you because I thought my sister loved you." My

brother said that he proceeded to beat the hell out of him.

When he was done, he could see the true person Joseph was - a

weak, pathetic man. "Anolese, he won't be bothering you

anymore." It took a while, but I finally found a permanent

place to live. I left my marriage with a few clothes and more

painful memories of abuse that I would have to live with.

When I moved into my apartment, I had nothing. I slept on the

floor with a pillow and a blanket, but I was away from the

abuse and I felt safe. I slowly tried to rebuild my life. I had

lost everything including my self-esteem. I'd endured the

physical abuse, but the verbal abuse would be the most painful, with a longer lasting mental affect. It took me twelve months to get out of my marriage, but the hell I endured would last for a lifetime.

I realized I was searching for Ryan in every man I met, but none of them had his kind heart. I told myself it was time for me to take a break from all men and be by myself. I had convinced myself I would be okay. I needed to get to know me again and to remember the values I was raised with. I had almost lost myself.

Chapter 5

I realized that I had to get back to my roots and remember everything that I'd been taught in Sunday school and the things that I was teaching others. I read a spiritual leader's declarations every day for thirty-one days. It was a reminder that God was helping me get through the things I was dealing with in my life.

I have always known how powerful God's favor is in my life. I had to remember that God said he would never leave or forsake us. For every wrong that happened to me in life, "I have never doubted that." God was making way for better things to happen to me. I believe he was also guiding me to help others deal with their problems. I realized I didn't have to tell all of my secrets, nor my pain and suffering in order to be a beacon for others. So I told myself that it was time to focus on my job at Quick Flash and try to forget about my past and look forward to my future.

I was at the grocery store one day and the male cashier said to me, "Hi Ms. Turner, you don't remember me, do you?" He told me his name and said, "You taught a class at my church on Interviewing Skills and how to dress and conduct yourself in an interview." He added, "It was the reason I got this job and I'm glad I have this opportunity to thank you."

I told him he was more than welcome and I was happy for him and I knew that he would go on to do great things. As I walked away, I felt good that I had helped someone. I have always known that God rewards you for the good you do in life. I know that for sure because I tested him. When I was about ten years old, my mother gave me my allowance for the week on a Saturday night. When I got to church on Sunday, the minister said, "It is better to give than to receive." He also said, "The more you give, the more God will give to you."

A Mother's Influence

After hearing him say those words, I decided to put my entire allowance in the collection plate. When I got to school on Monday, I didn't have any idea what I was going to do for lunch because I had no money.

Later that morning, one of my classmates came up to me and said, "My mom made me a bologna sandwich and I hate bologna. Do you want it?" I took that sandwich and washed it down with water and sat for a moment silently just to thank God for taking care of my needs on Monday and wondered what would be in store for the rest of the week. Needless to say, I ate lunch every day, whether that meant I found a quarter on the playground or someone offered me an apple. I realized that what I heard the minister say was the truth and I never forgot it. I became the person who would always try to do for others more than myself because I knew that God would always take care of me.

Every day at Quick Flash in Human Resources was unusual and exciting. I went to work with a plan but sometimes it didn't materialize. One day in particular, when I was preparing for a meeting and working on a project that was due in two days, a male employee came in to my office. He seemed troubled. I knew at that moment my plans were going to be derailed. He began by asking me questions which I knew didn't have anything to do with why he was really in my office. I could see that something was weighing heavy on him. I finally asked, "Dylan, why are you really here?"

Dylan said, "I have something very sensitive to talk with you about, but I'd rather do it off site. I was told by a few other managers that you are a very trustworthy person, honest and fair."

I said, "Thank you for the compliment. This is who I am, so I don't feel I can be anybody other than who I am."

A Mother's Influence

"Would it be possible for you to meet me offsite?"

Dylan continued to say that he had Wednesday off and if my

schedule permitted he would like to meet me at a coffee shop.

I asked, "Which one?"

"The Coffee Bean on Transit Road," he said. I

proceeded to give Dylan a time and told him that I would be

willing to meet him offsite. He left my office and I looked up

his information. I wanted to know who he worked for because

he was not a member of the unit I supported. Dylan's manager

was a very high ranking female executive who had only been

with the company three years. She had been climbing the

corporate ladder ever since she was hired. I tried to think of

what type of problem he could possibly have. He was a lower

ranked executive, himself. I put the information that I'd

gathered on him in my briefcase and I returned to working on

my project.

I met Dylan at the coffee shop and he began to tell me a story I would not have anticipated. Dylan told me that his manager had forced him to have sex with her to get ahead. Dylan said that he was very remorseful for betraying his wife and that he couldn't believe he allowed himself to be used like that again for a promotion. Dylan expressed to me that he was up for a promotion and had a conversation with his manager. He said she'd told him in no uncertain terms that, in order for him to get the promotion that he would have to sleep with her again. He told her that she was attractive, but he did not feel comfortable sleeping with her. He told me that he was more than qualified for the job and that he did not want to be unfaithful to his wife again.

I said to Dylan, "You should not have to sleep with her." I also told Dylan that it was what was called quid pro quo and everything that he told me was unethical. I told Dylan that I would have to speak with my supervisor and let her know what was going on.

A Mother's Influence

Dylan begged me not to tell anyone. He said, "Anolese, it has happened to others, I don't think the other two guys had a problem with it. I just needed to let someone know what the manager was doing." We ended the meeting after two hours of conversation.

After I got back to work, I scheduled a meeting with my senior manager. I was told in no uncertain terms to drop it and not to investigate. I was told that the manager was well liked, smart, and had sales that were off the charts and that her organization was a well-oiled machine and I should drop it. My senior manager said, "He's probably lying, just jealous because she's younger and is doing a fine job."

Something in me told me that Dylan was telling the truth. I think it took a lot of guts for someone to come forth with a story of that magnitude. I knew from my own experience with Joseph that I would have been better off, if I had told someone instead of carrying the guilt around with me.

I knew I had to help him. I met with Dylan again outside of work and asked him more specific questions. I had a long talk with him, documenting everything he was telling me. I had asked him questions several different ways and was getting the same answers. He told me his manager had made reservations at a hotel and she expected him to be there next Friday. He told me that he was going because it would mean more money for his family. I decided to go under cover. I knew that in order to expose this high level manager, I needed evidence. I didn't want to jeopardize my job without some concrete proof. I told myself not to form any opinions or conclusions until I had performed a thorough investigation. I was able to obtain a list of other employees from Dylan who could possibly corroborate the incidents in question. I couldn't believe my manager had given me so much push back and had emphatically said, "No." Dylan had also told me to drop it because he didn't want to get in trouble, even though he had given me so much information. But I just couldn't drop it.

A Mother's Influence

I decided to arrive at the Marriott Hotel a few hours before Dylan had to be there. I watched his manager walk up to the desk and check in. I snapped a picture of her with my camera. A few minutes later, Dylan walked in. You could tell by the look on his face that he was some place he did not want to be. I took a picture of him, as well. I also took pictures of them leaving separately an hour later. She looked gleeful. He looked sad and despondent. When I got back to work the next day, I contacted the HR manager for the executive and asked her if she would share a copy of the executive's expense report with me.

When I obtained the expense report several weeks later, I noticed that the hotel charge was on the bill. I said to myself, *that's a company violation. I got her!* A sense of accomplishment came over me. I looked up other employees in her department that had gotten a promotion within the last year and wrote down their names. I also noticed that Dylan was promoted a few days after their rendezvous.

I went home that evening and tried to determine my next course of action. I decided to schedule a meeting with the executive. When she walked into my office, I told her that I had a personal situation that I wanted to discuss with her that was off the record.

She said, "Sure, Anolese, not a problem."

I proceeded to tell her that I had uncovered a situation in her department. I told her that it had been brought to my attention that she had been demanding that her male employees sleep with her in order to get a promotion. I asked her, "Is it true? You might as well tell me the truth because I have proof."

She began by saying, "I don't believe I've done anything wrong. When I first got to this company, it happened to me and I just thought it was standard practice."

I asked her, "How did you feel the first time it happened to you?"

A Mother's Influence

She tearfully said that she was distraught and that she felt violated. She said she decided to push it to the back of her mind because she was good at her job. I reminded her that her employees felt the same way she had felt. She looked at me and asked, "What are you going to do?"

I told her that I was not trying to ruin her career but the behavior had to stop immediately. I opened a folder on my desk so she could see the photos that I had taken along with a copy of her expense report. I asked her, "What do you think I should do?" I told her I would give her a day or two to think about it.

Two days later, she walked into my office and showed me a copy of her resignation letter, which stated that she was leaving the company for personal reasons. She told me that she'd learned a powerful lesson and that it would never happen again.

The very next day, my senior manager came into my office and told me the executive that I had concerns about several weeks ago had just resigned and was leaving the company.

Barely keeping a straight face, I asked, "What was her reason?" "It was for personal reasons," she said.

I said, "What a loss."

My manager left my office.

Several days later, Dylan came into my office and asked, "What did you do?"

"What are you talking about?"

He said, "I know you did something. I don't know what, but thanks." Dylan walked out of my office with a look of gratitude on his face.

I just said, "Have a nice day."

It felt good to right a wrong. However, with all of the situations that I had to deal with at work and in my personal life, it was still taking a toll on me. I needed an escape and I yearned for the early days of my childhood when things were less complicated.

In Human Resources, as soon as you solve one problem, something else pops up. A few days later, I had just finished my lunch. Most days, I didn't have time to go out to lunch like other people because I always had so much to deal with. As I was sitting at my desk finishing my lunch, an employee tapped on my open door to see if I had a few minutes for a chat.

Graham started out by saying, "I don't know if there's anything you can do to help me, but I have a problem."

I told him to have a seat. "Graham, what's the problem?"

He put his head down and said, "Well, I'm losing my house because I'm behind in my mortgage and I can't afford the payments anymore. My wife is no longer in the picture. I was wondering if you could talk with my supervisor and convince him to give me more overtime."

I told Graham, "I have no authority over the scheduling of overtime for your department. My understanding is there is a standard process they follow to ensure that everyone is treated fairly."

Graham said, "I had to ask. I'm running out of options. The church has helped me with a payment and I have been doing a lot of praying lately." I don't usually talk about religion with my employees unless they bring it up. I told Graham, "It seems to me that you have a strong faith in God and I'm a true believer if something is meant to be, it will be."

In the story of Hebrews, the Bible teaches the importance of depending on God to carry man through times of struggles. The New Testament continues the theme of dependence on God during times of misfortune. Jesus in Matthew 11:28-30 says, "Come to me, all you who are weary and burdened, and I will give you rest. Jesus does not promise our life will be easy, but the burdens man encounters will feel lighter. All you can do is take your burdens to the Lord and leave them there. If you're going to worry, don't pray and if you're going to pray, don't worry.

I asked Graham if I could illustrate my point.

He said, "Yes, what do you mean?"

I said, "You have a really nice water bottle with you. When you take your burdens or problems to the Lord, you need to leave them there. So I want you to symbolize it by leaving your water bottle with me. This is where your faith comes in. Put your situation in God's hand and don't let it keep you awake at night."

He left his water bottle and thanked me for reminding him of the things he already knows. "Maybe I just needed to hear them again. Have a nice day, Ms. Turner."

"You too, Graham."

A Mother's Influence

A month later, Graham was in my office again. I was
sure he was there to give me news about his house. I didn't
know what I was expecting to hear. I do know that if something
is not meant for you, you won't have it. Graham told me that he
had an aunt down south that he didn't know that well and had
not seen in a long time. He said that she'd passed and left him
enough of an inheritance to pay off his mortgage. I told him I
was very sorry for his loss and I continued to say that God
moves in mysterious ways. I was both happy and sad for him. I
also handed him back his water bottle and told him to have a
nice day. He asked me if he could hug me and I agreed. When
he left my office, I thought to myself, *God's angels are working
overtime.*

Chapter 6

On a rainy day in the summer of 1984, the phone rang. I wasn't going to answer it because I was totally engrossed in a good book. After several rings, an eerie feeling came over me and I felt compelled to grab the phone. It was Mama and I could tell by her voice as she called my name that something was wrong.

Mama said, "Anolese, I have some bad news."

At that moment, my heart sank. I knew that my grandmother had passed. She was the only person in the family who had been sick. She'd been in a nursing home for several months. I thought back to the last time I'd seen her. It was the first week that she'd been placed into a nursing home. My mama had told me that grandma would not recognize me. But, as grandma glanced up at me, she said, "You are my granddaughter from New York." I knew my grandmother would remember me. I cried from the moment I heard the news of her passing. The loss affected me traumatically.

I loved my grandma more than words could ever express. She had my heart. My first year of college was at Reinhardt College in Waleska, Georgia, which was less than six miles from my grandparents' house. My grandfather worked on a farm and my grandmother cleaned homes and did other odd jobs in the community. She was always there for me.

Even though my parents weren't wealthy, they bought me a car to get back and forth to school. I could leave the campus for lunch. I would go to the campus canteen and pick up hoagie submarine sandwiches on Tuesdays and Thursdays and bring them to my grandparents. In exchange, Grandma would cook fried pork chops or fried chicken with biscuits and gravy. My favorites were chicken and dumplings and deep dish sweet potato cobbler. I loved everything that she cooked

A Mother's Influence

and my grandparents looked forward to the sandwiches I would pick up in the canteen at school and bring to them. Little did I know, those were the best days of my life. I lived with my parents off campus because they couldn't afford my room and board. However, I spent most of the time at my grandparent's house. My grandparents lived so close to campus that it was easy for me to stay with them when I had an early class or a late night. Most of the time, I just wanted to hang out with them. I couldn't imagine life without Grandma. She was the love of my life.

I remembered the times I spent the night and was able to go back to campus for parties. Grandma was special. She was not as strict as Mama. However, I would always have to be home by midnight. I never took advantage of Grandma's trust. Most nights, I was home before midnight. I was told I looked like my Grandma when she was a child. That always made me smile.

A Mother's Influence

After school, I would stop by my grandparent's house again. Grandma and I would sit and talk for hours. She would tell me about her childhood. Grandma and I had a special bond. Even though she was several decades older than me, she understood my problems and understood me. Grandma would always put me to bed after a glass of milk and a slice of sweet potato pie. I never told her that it gave me nightmares. I would always have some crazy dreams. My grandparents lived in the woods with no houses around, just howling coyotes. My mind would conjure up all kinds of horrible things in the middle of the night. I dreamt about bears breaking down the doors and carrying me off into the woods.

My sister and I made arrangements to fly home for Grandma's funeral. We arrived in Atlanta late. We rented a car and were just too tired to drive forty miles after working all day, so we decided to stay with one of my sister's girlfriends in Atlanta and drive to the funeral the next day.

A Mother's Influence

After my sister went to bed, my sister's girlfriend and I sat around the table and began reminiscing about loved ones and lost loves. I began to tell her about a guy named Ryan that I'd loved a long time ago. I told her about some of my relationships without revealing any of my secrets. My sister's girlfriend asked me if I had ever heard from Ryan. "No," I said. I told her that I'd spoken with his brother a few times over the years. She started talking about how life was too short and convinced me to call Ryan's brother and just have a casual conversation with him. I thought, what *the heck? What can it hurt?*

I made the phone call. Ryan's brother was genuinely happy to hear from me and asked if I had spoken with Ryan. I said, "Why would I do that? He's married."

His brother said, "Ryan got a divorce a year ago. I know he'd be happy to hear from you because he talks about you, but he didn't know how to contact you." Ryan's brother gave me his phone number and we ended our conversation with him saying, "Call him."

My past and future were flashing in front of my eyes. I wondered, *Should I call him? What if he's dating someone?* I knew the only way I was going to find out was to pick up the phone and call him. With mixed feelings of fear, anticipation, hope, girlish eagerness and despair, I finally grabbed the phone and dialed his number. I almost hung up, but I heard that very familiar voice, the same one that I'd heard over and over in my dreams. All I could say was "Hi, Ryan. This is Anolese."

He immediately took over the conversation, asking me, "Where are you?"

I told him that I was in Atlanta. "Where? What's the address?" he asked.

The next thing I remembered was a knock on the door and the door bell ringing. It was Ryan. I wondered how he'd gotten here so quickly. I later found out that he worked for the

Fulton Police Department and had used his siren. When I opened the door, my heart was pounding and I couldn't speak. He still had the same physique, and dimples and gorgeous smile. The man that I had wanted all of my life was standing before me and I couldn't utter a word.

Ryan said, "Anolese, it's so nice to finally see you again."

We embraced and I think we stood there holding each other for what seemed like hours. I don't think either one of us wanted to let go. I finally stepped back and invited him in. I introduced him to my sister's friend, who was very giddy. I don't think she could believe what was happening right before her eyes. I'm sure she must have felt the love between us. Ryan sat with us for thirty minutes, looked directly into my eyes and said, "I'm so happy you called me." Ryan told me that his brother called right before I did and told him to expect the surprise of his life. Ryan said, "I didn't know what my brother meant until the phone rang five minutes later and it was you."

Ryan asked, "Anolese, what brings you back home to Georgia? You seem happy, yet very sad."

I told Ryan that my grandmother had passed and I was here for her funeral.

Ryan said, "I remember how much your grandmother meant to you. Is there anything I can do?"

I said, "No, my sister and I have rented a car and we'll be driving up early tomorrow morning. Natalie went to bed early, so we can get an early start tomorrow."

After midnight, Janice whose house we were staying at, came back into the living room and said, "Goodnight, and Ryan, I'm glad I met you. Stay as long as you'd like, but if you're here when I wake up I expect breakfast."

A Mother's Influence

For most of the night, Ryan and I shared stories about our lives. I never wanted there to be any secrets between us. I said things to Ryan that most girls would never say to a man. I told Ryan that I found myself looking for him at my high school graduation ceremony. As I walked across the stage to accept my diploma, I scanned the crowd. Even though I knew in my heart it was impossible, I always had hope. I didn't know it was possible to love someone as much as I loved him. I realized at an early age that making love had very little to do with being in love. I told Ryan that when I finally left Georgia to visit my sister in Buffalo, I knew I was never coming back to Georgia to live and I never expected to see him again. I assumed that part of my life was over; especially after I heard he was married and had started a family. I told Ryan that I was looking for him in every man I met. I had wanted him to be my one and only. I told him about my job at Quick Flash and he told me that he'd been keeping up with me. He'd heard bits and pieces about my life from some of his friends in the old neighborhood. I told Ryan how I lost my virginity and sadness came over his face.

Ryan said, "I never wanted for any of this to happen."

I told him that it wasn't his fault.

Ryan said, "Anolese, I should have come looking for you after graduation. I wanted to. I just thought you didn't want me anymore and I knew you would never go against your parents' wishes."

We both cried in each other arms that night. Ryan told me that he would never leave me again and that he wanted to ensure that we would always be together. I wasn't quite sure what that meant, but I didn't ask any questions. He asked me if it would be okay for him to attend the funeral with me tomorrow. I said, "Yes." I told him the time and the church.

Ryan said, "Do you think your parents will have a problem with me being there?"

A Mother's Influence

I told him I didn't think so, that he was there for me and they would just have to accept it. As far as I was concerned, I didn't want him out of my sight again for as long as I lived.

Ryan left around three o'clock that morning, so I could get some sleep. Janice and my sister both woke up around 7:30 am. I could hear them stirring around the kitchen. I could smell the coffee brewing and I heard Janice say, "You missed some excitement last night."

As my sister was getting ready to say, "What do you mean?"

I walked into the kitchen.

I told my sister what had happened that night and, to my amazement, she was pleased. I asked myself, *had she secretly wanted us to be together?*

A Mother's Influence

We finished breakfast and decided to get on the road. My sister must have asked me a million questions about Ryan. "How do you feel about him after all this time?"

I told her that I've always loved him and knew that he was my one and only Prince Charming.

Natalie said, "You know we're only here for a few days. Are you going to spend any time with him?"

I told her that we hadn't talked about it, but that he was coming to the funeral.

Natalie said, "That should be interesting!"

I said, "Natalie, I'm older now and I can make my own decisions about my life…now more than ever."

When we arrived at my parent's house, everyone was getting ready. Mama hugged us both. My brother had arrived the night before. Mama said, "Girls, get ready. The limo will be here in two hours."

152

A Mother's Influence

Natalie asked, "Are you going to tell Mama about Ryan?"

I said, "No. Mama will see him when we line up to go into the church, because I want him to sit with me. They'll just have to deal with it."

"Anolese, you like living on the edge," Natalie said.

My grandmother's funeral was one of the saddest days of my life. I didn't have any more tears left. After the funeral, my mom came up to me and I said, "Mama, you remember Ryan."

She was actually quite courteous. Mama asked Ryan, "Will you be coming back to the house after the repast luncheon?"

Ryan said, "Yes, Ma'am, if it's okay with you."

Mama said, "Fine."

Ryan asked me if I would ride to the cemetery with him. I told my mama that I was riding with Ryan and she just shook her head with a "that's okay" look in her eyes.

After the repast luncheon, Ryan and I went for a long ride. When we returned to my parent's house, my mama said, "Where have you two been?"

I told her that I'd asked Ryan to take me out to Grandma's house and to Reinhardt College. I felt a desire to see those places again; the places that would bring back fond memories of my grandmother.

My parents had a casual conversation with Ryan. He stayed for a couple hours more before leaving for home. We talked on the phone later that night. Ryan asked me when I was leaving and if we could see me again. I told him that I didn't have a lot of time and that I'd be leaving in two days. He said that he'd be back tomorrow to take me out to dinner, if that was okay. I told him that would be great.

A Mother's Influence

The next day, I was so excited I could hardly wait. He must have been excited also because he arrived early. We went to the Willow Crest Hotel and Restaurant. The conversation flowed, as if we had never been apart from one another. After dinner, Ryan asked, "Anolese, can I come to see you when you get back to Buffalo?"

"Yes," I said. I could hardly contain my excitement.

Natalie and I said our goodbyes to our family and friends and headed to the airport. The first thing we had to do upon arriving at the airport was return the rental car. As we walked into the airport, I could see Ryan with a bouquet of daisies in his hand. I was excited to see him, but more than that I couldn't believe he remembered that they were my favorite flowers.

Ryan hugged and kissed me goodbye. "Anolese, I'll see you soon," he said.

When I boarded the plane, I took time to reflect on what had happened in the past five days. My grandmother had died, but it was as if she'd given me the gift that I wanted all my life. Being with Ryan had washed away all those painful years. I had come home for such a sad occasion, but I left Georgia with a heart full of hope that I could rebuild my life again - and with a promise from Ryan that he would be right by my side forever.

Chapter 7

Ryan had been flying back and forth to see me and had planned a special weekend for us in Niagara Falls. After we crossed the border, Ryan pulled up to The Embassy Suites Hotel and we checked into a room overlooking the falls. I had been to Niagara Falls many times. Every time family or friends came to visit, they always wanted to go to Niagara Falls. It had almost lost its appeal for me because I'd been there so often. However, this time was different. It was magical. The view from our room was breathtaking. We had lunch in the hotel dining room. When they seated us, I felt like we were sitting next to the waterfall. Ryan ordered for the both of us. I thought it was a very romantic gesture. He knew exactly how I wanted my steak cooked and that I wanted extra vegetables instead of a potato. It was the first time I experienced Niagara Falls as the city of romance.

A Mother's Influence

Niagara Falls is a city for lovers, a honeymoon retreat. It was a beautiful afternoon. As we walked along the falls, the spray was misting us. It felt great because it was about eighty degrees and the sun was shining brightly. As we looked up, we noticed a rainbow. There were families laughing and talking with their kids. There were food and souvenir vendors all around us. We stopped to sit down on a bench to take in the sights, sounds, smells and the beauty of it all. We decided it was time to return to the hotel to get ready for a night out on the town.

When we returned to the hotel, the manager stopped us in the lobby and said that our room had been changed because of a problem with the bathroom facilities. The manager proceeded to tell us that our belongings had already been moved. He handed us a new set of keys and told us that we would be a few floors higher and that he hoped the accommodations met our expectations.

A Mother's Influence

When Ryan and I got to the room, we immediately noticed that it was a suite; much larger, with a balcony. The sun was just setting and the lights had been turned on over the falls. It was a breathtaking view. There was a bottle of sparking wine chilling in a decanter. Ryan poured us a glass. He said, "Let's make a toast to a wonderful day."

I told Ryan that I felt like Juliet over looking her balcony.

He said he felt like Romeo. He smiled showing off his dimples. He kissed me so passionately and said, "Anolese, I have something to ask you. Will you marry me? I cleared it with your parents."

Even if he hadn't I would have said yes, and I did say yes! I had loved him most of my life and I knew he was my soulmate. I was truly the happiest girl in the world. I couldn't wait to get home and set plans in motion to quit my job at

Quick Flash and leave Buffalo to be with the man of my dreams.

Life was wonderful. Over the next year, we saw each other as often as we could. We spent holidays and vacations together. We spoke on the phone daily. Ryan would call me every night at 9:00 pm. Everything was perfect. Mama had finally come around and was warming up to the idea of me being with Ryan. I was finally going to end up with the man I loved and the man who loved me unconditionally.

I took my vacation and spent two weeks with Ryan at his apartment making wedding plans. One day after he had gone to work, his phone rang. I didn't think anything of it. I answered the ringing phone and it was his ex-wife. I told her he was at work. Later, I found out that she did not know about me. She found out that day from Ryan that we were engaged and were getting married within the next few months. After she found out about me, things got complicated. I don't think she was too happy. Ryan told me she frequently asked him to come over to her house to discipline the boys. I was cautious of his ex and her late night phone calls to Ryan. Being a woman, I could see through her deception. When someone finds out they are losing their ex to someone else, they can be conniving if they realize they left him for the wrong reason. They really don't want anyone else to have him. I told Ryan and he laughed it off. I knew she was up to something. *Maybe she divorced Ryan for all the wrong reasons?*

Ryan would continue to make his nightly phone calls to me, but the calls came later and later. Every time I asked him why he was calling so late, it would be because of his ex-wife. I could see that she was manipulating him and trying to weasel her way back into his life. I asked myself, why *can't he see it?*

Ryan and I were making plans for our upcoming wedding. Life was good for us until his mother became ill and was later diagnosed with cancer and only given a few months to live. Ryan loved his mother. He grew up without a father.

Nine o'clock would come and go with no phone call and I couldn't bring myself to call him. I knew something had changed and I didn't want to accept it, but I knew I had to deal with it. I contacted Ryan the next day to see why he hadn't called me.

Ryan said, "Anolese, this is the hardest thing I've ever had to do. The wedding is off. My mother's last dying wish was for me to promise her that I'd try to reconcile with my ex-wife, so I'm going to remarry her."

I knew Ryan loved his mother, but I didn't know to what extent he would go to please her. Another mother had successfully destroyed my life again and Ryan was to blame. *Can't he see what his mother has done to us...to me?*

I later found out that his manipulating ex-wife went to his mother and told her that she wanted Ryan back and that he should be with his children. Ryan remarried his ex-wife a few weeks before his mother died.

Just as I had given into my mother's wishes several years before, Ryan had given into his mother's wish. A mother's influence had separated us again. I felt as if my life was over and there was no reason to continue. I was devastated and overwhelmed with grief. All I wanted to do was end my existence. I called in sick for several days. I lay in bed awake for hours, unable to sleep. When I did get out of bed, I could barely hold my head up. I had no energy. The phone would ring and I wouldn't answer it. I couldn't go to work. I couldn't tell anyone I was an emotional wreck and couldn't function. I just had no energy left. I couldn't remember the last time I had a shower. All of my hopes and dreams were shattered. Those days I spent at home were days that I reflected on my life and everything that had happened to me. I was always in pain and couldn't see a way out. I felt hopeless; it was just too much pain to bear.

I decided to go to see Dr. Horne and share yet again the pain and disappointment that plagued me. I told him that my engagement had been called off and about the sleepless nights. I didn't want to reveal too many details. I think if I had, he would have sent me to a therapist or given me pills for depression. I wasn't ready to face the situation. I just wanted to stop the pain. What I really wanted was the doctor to give me something that would make me sleep forever. After my discussion with the doctor, he wrote me an excuse for work and gave me several prescriptions. I decided just to get the sleeping pill prescription filled. I stopped at a liquor store and bought several bottles of booze. One would have done the trick since I was not a drinker, but I wanted to make sure I had enough.

After I got home, I called my friends and family members, and talked with them for what would be the last time. Later, I started to prepare for my death. I made sure that my bedroom was clean and that I had on clean clothes. I don't know why I was thinking about such trivial things. I made

sure the pills and the booze were next to my bed. I got out all

of Ryan's letters and read them for the last time. I felt sorry

for myself. I wanted to remember what I'd lost. I put his

picture close to me. I wanted his face to be the last thing I saw

as I closed my eyes. I opened up the bottle of booze. I thought

it would give me the courage to take the pills. It was a Friday

night and I knew that no one would start looking for me until

Monday. After drinking half the bottle, I must have passed

out before taking any of the sleeping pills.

The next thing I remembered was waking up the next

day. I wondered why I was still alive. I looked over and the

pill bottle was empty and the booze was half gone. I got up

and stumbled to the bathroom. The entire house no longer

looked like a cave. All of my blinds and drapes were open. I

noticed my sister, Natalie, lying on the sofa asleep. When I

came out of the bathroom, she woke up and said, "Anolese,

when I talked with you earlier, I detected something in your voice and I couldn't shake it." She continued to say that when she got to my house and saw my car at home and I didn't answer the door, she knew something was wrong, so she let herself in with her key. She told me that she found me passed out and noticed the pills. She said she counted them to find out how many I'd taken. When she realized none were missing, she flushed them down the toilet. She said, "I knew you were intoxicated after seeing the bottle of whiskey half empty," so she decided to let me sleep it off.

My sister started with her, "No man is worth it speech." I didn't want to hear it. I told her she had no idea what my life had been like. "You're married to your childhood sweetheart. Life is good for you. You don't know anything about being single or alone. If Mama hadn't forbidden me to date or even see Ryan a long time ago, none of this would be happening to me now."

A Mother's Influence

"You have no reason to blame Mama. She only did what she thought was best. Anolese, you don't realize how she agonized over her decision. She didn't want the same thing that happened to her to happen to you."

"What are you talking about? Do you know something I don't? Tell me!"

"I can't tell you. I promised her I wouldn't."

"Oh well, keep your secret. I don't care anymore."

"Okay, Anolese, okay. I'm going to tell you a story that you will have to take to the grave with you."

Oh no, I thought. *Another secret.*

My sister explained, when I was eighteen years old, Mama took me shopping to buy clothes for college. She started off by saying that she loved us girls very much and that she had done the best she could to raise us. Knowing that I was going off to college, she couldn't protect me anymore.

Mama said she was about to tell me a story that she'd never told anyone and probably never would again but she said she felt the need to share it with me.

Mama said that she had a crush on an older man. She saw him at a football game and he walked over to her and started talking. She said it was a hot sticky humid night and he offered to buy her a soda. While walking to the concession stand, he realized that he'd left his wallet in his car. He asked Mama to walk with him. Mama said she didn't mind because she figured it would give them more time to talk. Mama said that she never expected what happened next.

"When they got to his car, he opened the front door pretending to look for his wallet on the floor. He reached back and opened the back door and asked Mama to look on the floor in the back to see if his wallet had fallen. When Mama leaned into the car, he pushed her down on the seat and raped her. He told her if she told anyone, bad things would happen to her.

A Mother's Influence

Mama said she never told anyone until now. I was going off to college and she wanted me to be careful of strangers and older men. Anolese, Mama wasn't trying to ruin your life; she was just being a mother."

"Why didn't she tell me?" I asked.

My sister said, "She had a hard time telling me the story." Mama probably didn't know how you'd react. I'm sure she didn't know you had carried around all this bitterness for her over Ryan.

"Over the years, Mama realized you had a very strong will and you knew what you wanted out of life at fifteen. Mama said she was saddened by not telling you. All she could remember was how this older man had taken advantage of her. Mama could see that you were enamored with Ryan. She thought it was just a crush and that you would get over him, but clearly you never did.

"Anolese, you can't keep blaming Mama. You need help dealing with your feelings and emotions. You need to somehow get past this. You need help, girl. If Mama knew you were going to try to commit suicide over Ryan, she'd be devastated. You mustn't ever tell her any of this!"

I told my sister that I had no plans of doing anything rash. I would never kill myself over a man. I wanted her to believe my story, even though I didn't believe it myself.

After that incident, Natalie watched me day and night until she thought I could be trusted again. I found myself daydreaming of my different relationships and all of the things I have had to overcome in my life and I realized I needed someone to confide in. I wondered if my friends or family would think I was weak, if they found out I was seeing a therapist. I always prided myself in being a strong woman, but I was losing my grip on reality. I told myself that I needed help and didn't care what others would think of me if they found out.

I contacted Dr. Horne and he gave me the name of a female therapist. I decided to schedule a session with her. When I met her, my defenses went up. I didn't get the right vibes from her. Basically, the only thing she said to me was, "Explain to me why you're here." She didn't ask any questions or make any comments, as I was explaining my situation. I didn't feel comfortable saying too much to her because there was no connection. I felt like I was talking into a recorder and I could do that at home. It was clear that we were brought up in two different places and culturally very different. I decided to cancel the next appointment. I didn't feel she was the right person to help me.

I then scheduled an appointment with Dr. Horne, my primary care physician, and explained to him what was going on in my life. He gave me the name of another therapist, one that he highly recommended. After I scheduled the appointment with the therapist Dr. Horne personally recommended, I received a medical history questionnaire in the mail. Right away, I could see how this therapist was different from the first one.

I sat down the day before the appointment and began to fill out the questionnaire. As I got to the section that asked if there was any mental illness in my family, I panicked. I started to ask myself, *Am I crazy? Could that be my problem? Am I mentally ill?* My mind started working overtime, cluttered with a flurry of thoughts. I realized that I couldn't sleep, didn't want anything to eat and didn't care if I lived or died. I wondered if I would one day wear the label of mental illness. I quickly put the questionnaire aside. The next day when I met the therapist, Kelli Jacobs, she seemed pleasant and comforting. As I walked into her office, I could see the infamous sofa and a big leather chair. I must have looked puzzled because she said, "Sit anywhere you'd like." She introduced herself to me. I asked her a few basic questions about her credentials and how long had she been in practice. Her first question was, "Did you get a chance to fill out the questionnaire?" I told her that I started, but couldn't finish. She said, "Can I see it? Let's talk about it."

"When I got to the section about mental illness, I freaked."

She said, "Why was that"?

I told her that I started to ask myself if I was mentally ill.

She said, "What I really wanted to know was has anyone in your family ever been diagnosed or hospitalized for any type of psychological or mental disorders, such as bi-polar or depression? Anolese, I don't think you're mentally ill. Let's just focus on what has been going on in your life. Why do you feel you need my help?"

I started to recap my first relationship and all the things that had brought me to this moment.

The therapist was easy to talk to. She made me feel at ease and I felt as if she was fully engaged and concerned about my well being. As I talked with her, she asked me questions. It was like a cleansing of the soul. It was extremely difficult for me to close my eyes and search through the folders in my mind of all the hurt and pain I'd endured in the life that I had already lived. There was so much pain and so much sorrow. It was draining to open up old wounds and have them analyzed and stitched back together. But it had to be done.

Over time, I was able to put all of my secrets on the table and deal with them. I hadn't realized that I'd blamed myself for so many things in my life. It was hard talking about them, but I was able to put everything in perspective. I realized I wasn't to blame for everything that went wrong in my life and neither was my Mama.

A Mother's Influence

After five months of twice weekly sessions, I began to feel whole again as I dealt with the blame and shame that I'd been carrying around. I was able to get on with my life. It had taken me a long time to mend my broken heart. I confided in a few friends and family about my situation. It felt good not to have secrets between us.

It had almost been a year. I decided that I'd never love a man again as much as I'd loved Ryan. I decided to close that door; Ryan was over.

I was focusing on my job and my life with friends and family when, out of the blue, I got a call from Ryan. I had nothing to talk with him about. If I had caller ID, I never would have answered the phone. Ryan told me that his mother had died almost a year ago. He had no idea that my parents had already told me. I expressed my condolences and was ready to hang up. He continued to tell me how sorry he was that he'd remarried his ex-wife, that he'd made a terrible mistake and had rectified his mistake.

I asked, "What do you mean?"

Ryan said, "I got a divorce again. I told my ex-wife that the only reason I remarried her was to appease my mother and that I didn't love her." Ryan said that he hadn't known she'd gone behind his back and convinced his mother to approach him about the remarriage. Ryan said that his mother was dead and the manipulation from his ex-wife had ended. Ryan began to tell me how much he still loved me and he still wanted to marry me.

Ryan was asking me to reopen a door I had painfully closed. He had no idea the pain I'd suffered. I was scared and couldn't put myself through this again. I told him that I was not in love with him and that I'd moved on. I ended by telling him to have a great life.

A Mother's Influence

When I hung up the phone, I didn't know how to feel. I knew I still loved Ryan, but he had no idea what I had gone through. I'd planned to kill myself over our relationship and the loss of his love. I knew I was not strong enough to go through another ordeal with him. I could not survive more rejection. I had no way of being sure it wouldn't happen again. I was going to give up on the man I loved because I had become weak where he was concerned. It had taken many months of therapy to get to where I was and another step back would push me over the edge.

I contacted my therapist and met with her to explain what had happened.

My therapist listened without saying a word. She asked me, "Do you still love him?"

I said, "Yes." I told my therapist that she'd helped me close a door that I wanted to remain shut, but I was now questioning whether I should have left it open. I told her that I was afraid to allow Ryan back in my life, since I realized I hadn't gotten over him. I also told her I had taken the cowardly way out. I didn't want to take the risk of having another relationship with Ryan and possibly get hurt all over again. I told her that I sat alone with memories of what could have been.

Chapter 8

One day, while standing outside my manager's office waiting for him to get off the phone, I overheard him say that he had an immediate need for a Human Resource Manager to work in Dallas for a year. I knew at that moment none of my co-workers would volunteer for such an assignment; they all had families. I was the only one in the group without a life; no husband, no children, not even a boyfriend.

I knew it would probably take my manager a while to ask me, so I decided to be prepared. I started to jot down all the things I would ask for, if he approached me. At the top of my list was more money and an alarm system for my current house. I wanted to live in a gated community and my new residence would also have to have an alarm and at least two bedrooms to accommodate my friends and family when they wanted to visit. I wanted to be able to fly home every two weeks. I figured my list included things he wouldn't go for and I had reservations of whether I wanted to leave my comfort zone and experience the challenge of the unknown. It took my manager, James, several days, but he walked into my office on a Friday afternoon and stated that he had an assignment for me that would probably mean a promotion in the future.

James, who we secretly called Jimmie because he had a boyish smile and was very good looking, said, "Anolese, I need for you to temporarily relocate to Dallas for a year. That plant is being closed and the senior human resource manager, Sabrina, is being relocated. We need someone with strong people skills to be the glue that holds the plant together during this transition period." James added, "I don't need your answer today, but I would like to know by Monday."

I told James that I didn't need to think about whether I wanted to take the job or not. I was willing. However, I asked him if I could have a few hours to think about what I might

A Mother's Influence

need to prepare myself for the move and I'd give him my final

answer with any conditions that I might have. I told him I was

honored that he thought I was the right person for the job. I

tried not to appear overly excited. I had already made out my

list, but I didn't want him to know because then he would

know I had overheard his conversation.

I met with James before the end of the day. I told him

I had a few requests.

James immediately asked, "What are they?"

I rattled off my request and gave him the list.

He told me that he'd give them some thought and get

back to me on Monday.

All I thought about that weekend was moving to Dallas

for a year. I weighed the pros and cons. I had moved out of

my first house after living there for fifteen years because I had

been held up at gun point. It had changed my life. I knew the neighborhood was taking a turn for the worst, but it was my first house and it almost paid for.

I remember the day I was robbed like it was yesterday. I'd been sick all weekend. The day it happened, I was trying my best to get over the flu, but I knew no matter what I had to be well by Monday, the next day. I had meetings that could not be rescheduled. I didn't have any Nyquil or Tylenol for my fever, or stockings for the outfit that I'd planned to wear, so I decided to go out and purchase them. When I returned home, parked my car and started to get out, a gun was pointed at my forehead. I thought I was going to die that evening. I could feel the coldness of the gun barrel. It was two guys and they demanded money. I managed to say, "I don't have any money." For an instance, I thought, that *No one carries cash anymore; we all use ATM cards.* They saw my cell phone and my car keys, and grabbed them and proceeded to snatch my glasses from my face. In the distance, we could see bright lights coming toward us. In the distance, you could tell that it was a car. As we all watched, the car approaching blinded me.

It must have frightened them. At that very second, they saw

my purse strap under my coat and around my neck and began

to tug on it. The strap broke and they yanked it so hard that

they were pulling me out of the car with it. I tried to flag down

the car, but when it passed I didn't see anyone in the driver's

seat. I couldn't believe that I had survived the ordeal. Even

though they took my purse, I still had my life. I found my car

keys in the street where they'd dropped them in their haste to

get away. I went into the house and called the police.

When the police came and questioned me, I felt

violated all over again when they put me in the back of the

police car and drove me around to try to find and identify the

suspects. I knew I should have moved from that neighborhood

years earlier. There were times when I would come home from

work and couldn't drive down my own street or get to my

house due to a shooting, a stabbing, or a home invasion. My

house was almost paid for. I didn't think I could afford a

house in the suburbs, so I tried to protect what I had. I put an alarm on my house and thought everything would be okay. Little did I know that this terrible crime would take place right outside my home. I loved my home, but after this incident my house was no longer a home. It had been remodeled on the inside and outside and didn't need any more work. It would have been paid off in less than two years.

After being held up at gun point, I left my house that evening and didn't return until three months later and then just to pack my belongings and sell the house. I no longer felt safe anywhere. It had taken me a while, but I had finally found a HUD house in the suburbs that I could afford. It was extremely hard in the beginning to pay two mortgages. I had no idea that was even possible on my salary. I realized that God had saved me and he must have something greater in store for me. *He is the only one that can make a way out of no way.*

A Mother's Influence

I figured that living in Dallas would give me the opportunity to have work done on my new house because it wasn't yet livable and I didn't have the money to stay somewhere else. I just wanted to have a contractor oversee the work on the house and I planned to come home every other week to check on the progress.

I'd begun to look forward to the change in scenery. I told myself that the change would do me good. I couldn't wait to hear if my requests would be honored.

On Monday morning when I arrived at work, I checked my voice mail. James had left me a message saying that he needed to see me immediately. I hung up the phone, got a cup of coffee -which was on the way- and proceeded to his office.

Again, he was on the phone. I thought to myself that I had overheard enough of his conversations lately, so I decided to leave him a note and tell him I would be in my office for another hour before I began my day of meetings. It didn't take James long.

It was a matter of minutes before he appeared in my office doorway. "Anolese," he said, "I had a conversation with my manager and the relocation department. I'm sure we can grant all of your requirements for the assignment in Dallas. However, we need you to leave in two weeks. I've scheduled an appointment for you to go over all the details with the Relocation Department. I've asked one of the other managers to take over your current assignments and meetings, so that you can focus on getting ready for the move. By the way, the current manager from the Dallas office will be here tomorrow to discuss her new assignment with me, so you'll be able to meet her."

I was speechless. I got through the rest of the day not remembering what I had done all day because I was so excited.

A Mother's Influence

After I got home, I looked around the house and began taking inventory of all the things that needed to be done. I made a list just to prioritize what had to be done immediately and what could wait. I thanked God I didn't have to live here during the renovations.

I remember the day I saw the sign in the window of the HUD house I'd purchased. Samantha and I toured it with a realtor. The house was in such bad shape, but I was visionary. I put a bid on the house, but I had to wait for weeks to see if my bid had been accepted. I called the phone number I was given for several weeks and eventually found out that I'd won the bid. One of the things that I didn't know at the time was that Samantha had gone home and told her husband that she wouldn't have allowed her dog to live in that house and she didn't know why I was even considering it. Years later, she told me that her husband had told her not to burst my bubble and to keep those thoughts to herself. I admit that the house needed a lot of work and most of that work had to be done before I could get a mortgage.

Most of the dry wall in the house had to be replaced due to all of the holes in the walls. It needed new doors in every room. It looked as though someone had kicked holes in them. All of the floors had to be replaced. Since I hadn't owned the home at the time of making most of the repairs, I wasn't able to get the water turned on. The guys who worked on the home brought in their own water to mix the dry wall compound.

After a while, I asked the real estate company to have the water turned on in their name and they reluctantly agreed. I met the water man at the house on my lunch hour. He immediately had to turn the water off again because we could hear water running in the walls. The same guys that put up the drywall had to take it down, so they could get to the water leaks. They eventually told me that there were thirty seven water leaks. I did a lot of crying during the days when I first purchased the house.

There were no light fixtures in the house, so I had to purchase them. I was slowly seeing my dream of living in a safer community become a reality. I finally had to have the furnace checked. The day the gas man came to check out the furnace he turned on the gas. Samantha and I were upstairs in a bedroom removing nasty wall paper off the walls and we smelled gas. I ran downstairs to tell the gas man and he said that it was natural to smell gas because the furnace hadn't been on in several years. I insisted he walk upstairs with me and smell it for himself. He immediately told us to get out of the house. He went around the house to the meter and could tell there was a problem. He told us to ask the neighbors on each side of my house to leave their property due to the danger of a gas explosion. He turned the gas off and started checking various places for gas leaks. He went into the laundry room and was able to see that there was no cap on the gas pipe that would have connected the dryer. The gas man thanked us for being persistent with him. He had no idea that we could have died that day if Samantha and I weren't trying to quit smoking and if it wasn't our first day of going without a cigarette. I told myself, *God has intervened again.*

I remembered standing at the top of the stairs in my new home and saying to myself that in my lifetime, I'd given so much to so many as wedding gifts, baby shower gifts, and birthday gifts. I stood there unmarried, no children and no reason for anyone to do anything for me. Little did I know that God had planned to give me back double, even triple, the things that I'd given others. I stood there at the top of those steps crying and rejoicing over the goodness of God through others. It became abundantly clear that God loved me and was protecting me. Two months later, I closed on the house and it was mine.

A Mother's Influence

I wanted to go to Dallas and I didn't want to go Dallas.

What have I done? I was overwhelmed. My entire life was about to take on another drastic change. I found myself displaying various emotions of joy, sadness and loneliness. However, I had made my decision, so I needed to snap out of it. I needed to make arrangements to take care of my household affairs. Everything was happening so fast.

I decided to grab a few minutes of solitude, so I sat down on the sofa. I had just put my feet on the ottoman when the doorbell rang. I got up and walked downstairs to the door and opened it. Melissa, my friend, was standing there with two tea bags in her hand. *How does she know that it's the only thing missing from my quiet time?*

"Anolese," Melissa said, "I have had the day from hell and nothing's gone right. Let's have a cup of tea."

As we walked up the stairs to the kitchen, I was asking myself if I should tell her about my day and my decision to relocate for one year. I didn't want to make things worse for her; we had become such good friends since I moved into the neighborhood, but I knew I couldn't keep these emotions to myself. I decided to wait until she had her cup of tea. I also checked the kitchen for some comfort food. I found several slices of lemon pound cake that I'd taken from my sister's house after our Sunday dinner.

During Melissa's second cup of tea, I decided to break the news. "Melissa." I said, "I have some news of my own."

Melissa said, "Okay, Anolese, let me have it. After the day I've had, I can handle anything. Your news can't be as bad as my day was."

I said, "Melissa, Quick Flash is sending me on a temporary assignment for a year to Dallas, Texas."

"What? I can't believe it! We have just gotten to know each other. Do you realize you're the only person I talk to? When are your leaving?"

A Mother's Influence

"I'll be leaving in two weeks."

Melissa was shocked. She asked, "Why so soon?"

"The manager who is currently there has taken another position. I'm somewhat apprehensive about the idea of leaving, but I know it is the right thing to do at this point in my life and it will be good for my career."

"Anolese, I'm sure that you know what's best for you. I'm happy for you. I'm going to try to look at the bright side, another vacation spot for me. Is there anything that I can do to help you?"

"I'm trying to figure out how I'll get work done in the house while I am away."

Melissa said, "I can let the contractors in for you. I'll make sure the work gets done to your satisfaction. I'll come over and have a cup of tea at your house; give you a call on your phone in the evenings on the worker's progress, and it won't cost me a dime." Melissa smiled.

"You're funny, Melissa, but I kind of like the idea. As part of the relocation package, Quick Flash will be installing an alarm system on the house and a house watch service will be doing the outside chores. If you're serious, I'll introduce you to the representative tomorrow when he arrives. I'll explain that you'll have a key and the code so you can look after the house, as well."

As Melissa was walking down the steps toward the door to leave, she looked back and said, "I've heard enough news for today. I think I'll go home, take a sedative and get a good night's sleep. Let's plan to have tea early tomorrow, so we can sort out the details."

I looked at Melissa, walked towards her and gave her a hug. "Thanks for being my friend." I closed the door, walked up the stairs and glimpsed at the clock. It was

A Mother's Influence

nine o'clock on a Friday night and I was going to be alone. *I see why I was the boss' first choice for the assignment. I don't have a life.* I told myself, *you'll meet someone in Dallas* I laughed out loud and got ready for bed.

I was so happy that Melissa and the house watch guy, Brian, got along so well. Brian looked like a hippy. He was very tall, skinny, had an earring in both ears and a nose ring. Brian sounded very credible and explained everything fully. He stated that the alarm system would be installed the next day.

During the winter months, the driveway would be plowed and the sidewalks cleaned and during the summer months, the grass would be cut once a week. Even though Melissa would have her own alarm code, she was required to inform Brian every time she entered my house due to the monitoring of the alarm.

My next steps were to inform my family and friends that I was leaving for a year. I knew I had to call my parents. Mama and Dad wouldn't notice the difference because we didn't live in the same state. It would be more difficult for the rest. I decided to phone my brother; a personal visit was not necessary. He would be overjoyed, what I really mean is he would be jumping for joy that he didn't have to help me with the yard work. My sister, Natalie, on the other hand, was the one I dreaded telling. I knew she would miss me more because we talked on the phone every day and I was at her house several times a week. Natalie was saving for retirement, so I knew that I'd have to call her. She was frugal – there was no way she would make frequent long distance phone calls. I decided to go to her house and tell her in person.

I told my friends I was leaving for a year and they wanted to know the address and how soon they could visit. I didn't expect to be lonely any time soon. I expected my weekends to be busy entertaining friends and family.

A Mother's Influence

I glanced out the window and the thermostat read twenty-five degrees. It was colder than I thought and it had just begun to snow. For a moment, I closed my eyes and imagined how warm it would be in Dallas. I put my coat and boots on, ran downstairs and went into the garage. I got in my car and thanked God that I didn't have to brush off the snow. Knowing that I was leaving Buffalo for a year gave me a better appreciation of the beauty of the fresh fluffy snow on the trees. It looked like powdered sugar covered the grass.

As I approached my sister's house, her husband, Roger, was outside using the snow blower to clean the driveway. I beeped the horn and waved. I dashed into the house. I took my boots and coat off and dropped them. I could feel the warmth of the fireplace. I went into the family room and Natalie was asleep in her recliner.

She had bought a recliner for Roger for Father's Day and decided that he looked too comfortable; so she went out and bought one for herself. She looked so peaceful I decided not to wake her. I went into the kitchen and opened the fridge. It was almost lunch time and I was hungry. Someone had done some winter barbecuing. It could have been Natalie or Roger, they both loved to cook. There were ribs, chicken and corn on the cob. I took one of each. I was sitting in the family room lounging on the sofa when Natalie awoke and asked, "How long have you been here?"

I told her what I always tell her, that she sleeps too sound. I could have been a burglar.

When she was fully awake, I told her that Quick Flash was temporarily relocating me to Dallas for a year and that I was leaving next weekend. Natalie looked at me with her mouth wide open, but nothing came out. Natalie finally said, "Anolese, am I still dreaming? Are you kidding me?" She had a flurry of questions.

A Mother's Influence

I finally said, "Natalie, I know this is sudden, but it's something that I want to do and I need a change of scenery." I sat with her for a few hours assuring her that I'd be fine. Although she didn't take the news well, when I told her that I would see her every two or three weeks she stopped being so inquisitive.

When I arrived at home that evening, I decided to call my parents. Telling them was uneventful. For them, basically nothing would change. I would still be about thirteen hundred miles away. I would continue to call them, no matter where I was located. I overhead Dad saying to Mama, "Honey, we'll have another vacation spot which would be a lot warmer."

I told Mama that I heard what Dad said and he was right.

Dad said, "When will you be settled? I'm looking forward to planning a trip to visit you." I told Dad to give me a few weeks.

My manager informed me that it would be okay to take someone with me on my house hunting trip. I asked my best friend, Samantha, if she wanted to tag along, and she was excited to go with me. Samantha could work from the Dallas office and not have to use any vacation time.

It took forever to get to Dallas. There were no direct flights from Buffalo. We had to change planes in Chicago. We were in the air for about six hours. I see why my manager agreed to fly me home every two weeks. They probably knew I would not make that journey every two weeks and, if that's what they counted on, they were right.

After Samantha and I got off the plane, we rented a car and started the forty minute ride to the hotel. After checking in, I called the plant, and Sabrina, the HR Manager from the Dallas office, came to our hotel and took us to lunch. After lunch at La Madeline's, we went condo hunting.

A Mother's Influence

Quick Flash's relocation department had given me the names of several places to check out. They were all in posh neighborhoods. I settled on one in Plano, which was about ten miles from the plant. I later found out that what I thought would be a short ride to work turned into a forty five minute drive because of the traffic.

After finding a place to live, I still had time to visit the plant. It was a small facility compared to Quick Flash's home office in Buffalo. The employees and staff seemed friendly. After sizing up the plant, I decided to tour the city. It was nice of my manager to let Samantha travel with me, so I wouldn't have to be alone in a strange city. Samantha could only stay with me for a few days, so we went sightseeing as often as possible. I was still staying in the hotel when Samantha left to go back to Buffalo.

Chapter 9

I started the assignment, checked out of my hotel and moved into my condo the following Monday. I was excited. The outgoing manager introduced me to the leadership team which was comprised of twelve managers. The transition went very smoothly. I scheduled individual meetings with the leadership team members and got to know each of them. It took a couple of weeks for us to finalize action plans for the shutdown of their various departments. I'd been there a few weeks and had gotten to know most of the employees and staff. They seemed nice. In the back of my mind, I was sure the employee's attitudes towards me would change when they found out the real reason I was there.

When the closure was announced, I didn't get the reaction I'd expected. There had been rumors that the plant would eventually close, which meant the employees were

A Mother's Influence

expecting the announcements. Employees were already leaving at a rapid pace, finding jobs at other companies. Dallas was a metropolis with many companies moving in every day due to tax breaks.

After several weeks of being at the office for ten and twelve hour days, I needed to relax. I slept late on Saturday mornings and got up around ten o'clock to get ready for a day of sightseeing. I wanted to see what Dallas had to offer. I took long drives touring the city, using my GPS to find different points of interest. I talked to a few people back in Buffalo. One of them happened to mention that she had a sister who lived about an hour away from where I was living and asked me if it would be okay to give her sister my phone number. After a week, I got a call from her sister, Taylor, and we agreed to meet at my condo in Plano. That was the beginning of a great relationship. We immediately hit it off and spent a lot of time together and became friends. She was married with identical twins; two gorgeous girls, Catherine and Chloe, who were six years old.

As we got to know each other better, I gave her a key to my apartment. Her husband had a few days off during the week and would bring the girls to my condo to go swimming in the pool. Taylor and I would go shopping and she would invite me to various outings with her and her friends. Taylor lived about an hour from my condo, but we managed to see each other every couple of days because she worked thirty minutes from me. Sometimes, we'd meet for dinner. She became a big sister to me, even though I was much older than her. She called often to check on me. After meeting Taylor and her family, I didn't feel the need to go home as often. I wasn't alone anymore.

Most of the places Taylor took me to I was later able to find on my own when my friends came to visit. We toured the Book Depository Museum where Lee Harvey Oswald was accused of shooting President Kennedy. It was an eerie feeling being in the same room where Lee Harvey Oswald stood when he shot the president. I felt as though I was reliving my parents' memories, as they spoke of those days. My mama told me that she and Dad sat in front of the black and white television for hours. It felt as though they'd lost a member of their family. As Mama and Dad talked about President Kennedy's death over the years, I could sense sadness in their voices and eyes which looked as if it penetrated their hearts. I wondered why this man had such an effect on them. They'd never met him and didn't know him personally. Years later in life, I came to realize his effect on the country. Standing there amongst the memorabilia, I felt the same sense of loss they must have felt.

It was a treat when Taylor took me to visit the South Fork Ranch where some of the show "Dallas" was filmed. The house was very small in comparison to what we saw on television, as they actually filmed in a studio in Hollywood. I toured the mini museum and the gift shop. I bought several little trinkets for my friends. I loved watching "Dallas." It was a ritual for me and my friends to watch and then call each other to discuss what we'd just seen. We couldn't wait to find out who'd shot JR.

I also had an opportunity to go to the South Fork ranch for a huge picnic. The Caterers had cooked a variety of meats for the picnic and that day I discovered my love of brisket. From that point on, I was hooked on barbecue. It had become a staple in my diet while in Dallas.

Shopping was a favorite past-time of mine. I shipped many things back to Buffalo to help furnish my new home. Dallas had stores that Buffalo didn't have, such as World Market, Ross, Garden Ridge and too many more to name. I loved to decorate, so everything that was unusual and I liked, I shipped back.

A Mother's Influence

When my friends and family came to visit, I was able to take them to the places I had visited. I drove my friends to the neighborhoods where some of the Dallas Cowboys lived. One of the Dallas Cowboys had a huge gate in front of his property which read "PRIME TIME." It was a gorgeous house from the outside and it took up almost a block. I had no idea at the time that Deion Sanders lived there. It surprised me that they didn't live in gated communities.

I attended a rodeo and went to some of the famous bars in the Fort Worth Stockyards. I'd never seen so many people wearing cowboy hats and boots, except for shows on television. One weekend, I even drove to Shreveport, Louisiana to a casino to play the slot machines. It was built close to the waterfront. I'm not a gambler. I was doing more sightseeing than anything. After my allotted twenty dollars was gone, it was time for me to leave. I had a great time, but I'd rather spend my money on the things I could still own years later.

A Mother's Influence

I did a lot of sightseeing and I loved going to the flea markets. When I heard about a large Flea Market in Mason, Texas I couldn't wait to go there. One Saturday morning. Taylor and I left home early for the Flea Market in Mason which was about an hours drive away. As we were driving along listening to music, we heard a noise and knew right away we had a flat tire. I called AAA and they told me it would take several hours for them to arrive. We were both disappointed because it meant less time at the market and possibly all the good stuff would be gone when we arrived. I decided to be daring and wave my hands to see if I could flag down a car. Several cars went past without stopping. A few minutes later, a guy in a red Mustang stopped. After being so bold, I was suddenly a little apprehensive, but I managed to ask him if he could change the flat tire for us.

He said, "Yes."

A Mother's Influence

After he'd agreed, I said, "Thank you. My name is Anolese and this is my friend, Taylor."

He said, "My name's David. Are you ladies from around here?"

I didn't want to give him too much information. I told him that I was in Dallas on a business assignment.

David asked, "How long will you be in Dallas?"

I said, "Several months."

Taylor spoke up and said, "I live here."

David continued to make small talk.

I could tell that he was trying to get up the nerve to ask me more personal questions. He had a sticker on his car that read, "American Red Cross Volunteer." When he was finished, I offered to pay him, but he refused the money. He handed me a business card and I stood there for a moment having a conversation with myself. My inner voice was saying, *why don't you just give him a fake number?* Then the voice said, *you can't do that. That's not who you are.* I was not going to give him the number to my condo, so I gave him my business card which only had my office phone number on it. There was no way I was going to give him my cell number. I wasn't sure if I really wanted to be bothered.

David said, "Maybe I can take you to lunch one day?"

I said, "That would be nice."

We said our goodbyes and got back on the road, so that we could continue our shopping trip. Taylor talked about how bold I was and that was something she would have never done. I asked Taylor to call AAA and cancel the service call. If I hadn't stopped David, we would still have been waiting in the hot sun.

The following Monday when I returned to work, David had left me a message. "Anolese, it was nice meeting you and Taylor. I'd like to get to know you better. Would it be

210

A Mother's Influence

possible for you to meet me for lunch one day this week? Call me back and let me know."

I didn't call him back that week, even though he left several other messages. I'd mentioned the encounter to one of my co-workers and they said, "Anolese, I'm sure he's harmless. I'll go with you, if you want me to."

Since my co-worker had agreed to go with me, I finally gave in and met him for lunch. It was the least I could do since he changed my tire.

I called David and apologized for not returning his many phone calls. I told him that I'd been extremely busy due to the magnitude of the assignment I was on. I arranged to meet him at a Mexican restaurant which was down the street from my office. My co-worker tagged along and I introduced her to David. I told him that she'd asked me what I was doing for lunch and I hoped he wouldn't mind that I brought her with me.

David said, "Of course not."

I was glad my co-worker came with me because she was very inquisitive. She began to ask David all sorts of questions. I found out where he lived, worked and hung out most of the time. My co-worker also wrote down his license plate number when he left. She looked at me as we were leaving the restaurant and said, "Anolese, he seems harmless - I'll know more about him before the end of the week."

David turned out to be a really nice guy. I spent a lot of time with him. I eventually introduced him to Taylor's husband. We all got along so well.

My assignment consumed me. I worked a lot of twelve hour days and I also played hard. I was busy every day and every weekend. I was four months into a one-year assignment.

This assignment was the first time that I'd been excited about work and having a life.

A Mother's Influence

During the sixth month of my assignment, word started to leak to the employees that the business was closing and more and more employees were leaving at a rapid rate. We had different vendors walking in and out of the building constantly because we tried to ensure that we were able to sell off all of the equipment.

Even though David and I had a great time together, I wanted to do things without him and I could tell that was a little unsettling for him. He wanted to monopolize all of my time.

As I began to meet other people and told David that I was doing things with others that I'd met, he would say, "Is that your way of not spending time with me?"

I told him that I'd just made other plans and if he wanted to, we could do something the following weekend. I wasn't aware at that time how insecure he was. We'd been hanging out as a couple for several months. He'd become a hangout buddy for me. We went on several weekend trips to Austin and Houston.

I had always insisted that we stay in separate rooms and that I'd pay for my own room. I thought by paying for my own room, I was making myself clear that we would not have a sexual relationship. We went out to dinner a lot and I would also insist that we split the bill. I was having a great time until I could tell that he was more serious than I was. I started to back away and not see him as often. One evening, he showed up at my house with a huge teddy bear, flowers and a proposal. He got down on one knee and asked me to marry him. I was shocked. We hadn't talked about marriage. I thought, *where is this coming from?* I knew I couldn't accept his proposal, but I was trying very hard to figure out how to tell him without hurting his feelings. Needless to say, I didn't accept his ring and he was heartbroken. He stormed out of the condo. He didn't call me for several days and I made no attempts to call him.

A Mother's Influence

When David's disappointment subsided, he continued to profess his love for me and said that even though I was leaving Dallas he was not going to give up. I told him I was truly sorry if I'd misled him in any way. I was not interested in a relationship. I thought I'd made that clear every chance I got. I hated the fact that he'd fallen in love and I hadn't. I've known that feeling of unreciprocated love and heartbreak.

I had one month left on my assignment and had begun to plan my vacation before returning to cold Buffalo. I decided since I was so close to California that I should fly to San Francisco, a city I'd always wanted to visit. I went online and started to map out all the points of interest that I wanted to see. I went ahead and purchased my plane ticket, reserved a rental car and secured a hotel room right in the heart of everything in Union Square. I wanted to be close to shopping and specialty shops. I'd begun to feel both sadness and excitement about the end of my assignment and my seven day vacation. I decided that I'd drive across the Golden Gate Bridge; take a ride on the blue and gold fleet for a day trip to visit Alcatraz; take a ride on the famous Cable Cars; drive down the winding road of Lombard Street; have dinner at Pier 39, the famous Fisherman's Wharf, and Visit Chinatown.

After making all of my vacation arrangements, I was able to focus on closing the office and do all the last minute details that went along with leaving.

Every night after work, I went home and packed a few things to make sure that I was ready to move out on the day I was supposed to because I was flying out the day of my move.

My assignment was nearly over and the leadership team and some remaining employees decided to take me out to lunch for the last time.

My assignment had come to an end. Any remaining details would be handled by the managers who were left to close the plant. I'd already processed all of the necessary paperwork for the remaining staff and employees. They gave me a great

216

A Mother's Influence

send off with flowers and a gift card for my favorite store, T J

Maxx. I guess the word had gotten around because when

someone asked me what I did during my weekend when not at

work, it often included going to T J Maxx, Marshalls or

HomeGoods. Even though the assignment had been grueling, I

enjoyed my time in Dallas.

Taylor invited me to dinner my last evening in Dallas.

We decided to meet at a restaurant in Plano. She didn't want me

to have to drive far due to the fact that I was leaving town the

next day. She took me to my favorite restaurant in Dallas where

I could eat as much brisket as I wanted. I had such a great time

with her family that evening. They gave me a going away gift,

which was a picture of their family for me to remember them by.

I extended an invitation for them to visit me back in Buffalo

because her sister was planning to move out of state. I told them

my doors were forever opened to them because they'd become

like family to me. It was a very tearful goodbye.

A Mother's Influence

When I turned in my key at the condo office, I gave the receptionist the beautiful flowers I was given because they were still gorgeous and I couldn't take them with me.

When I arrived in San Francisco, I became aware of the fact that I was alone and found myself wishing I'd asked a girlfriend to meet me there. However, the adventure would have also been romantic if I had a boyfriend who could have been by my side. I was determined to make the best of my adventure. When I got off the plane, I went directly to the rental agency to pick up my car to begin the last leg of being away from home for almost a year. I found my way to my hotel in Union Square, where I was told I would be close to everything. I don't remember who gave me that advice, but they didn't steer me wrong. I checked into my hotel, not realizing how exhausted I was. I wanted to immediately unpack and begin my tour of the city. Unfortunately, I was both mentally and physically exhausted. I took a shower and sat down on the bed. I don't even remember falling asleep, but when I woke up it was five

218

A Mother's Influence

hours later and I realized I was in a different time zone. I think
it was my brain's way of releasing all of the stress of the past
year, so I could concentrate on my vacation and have a good
time. When I finally awoke, it was four o'clock in the morning
and I called downstairs and asked for an eight o'clock wake up
call. *I told myself, that'll give me enough time to be up and
dressed by ten to begin my day.*

I was a little apprehensive but I hopped on the cable cars
off of Lombard Street. It was a great mode of transportation,
especially for sightseeing. I purchased a one day pass so I could
stay on the cable cars as long as I wanted to. After two hours, I
hopped of and got on another one going in the opposite
direction. While riding, I stood holding on to the overheard bar
for a while until I was able to get a seat. I was right up front, not
far from the conductor. It was fascinating how he went through
several steps to brake. Going down hills was my favorite
because it felt like I was on a roller coaster. I got off where I had

originally boarded, so I could keep my bearings. It was a great way to start my sightseeing adventure.

After returning to the hotel, I was exhausted so I decided to call room service. I had dinner in my room and put my itinerary together for the next day of sightseeing. I was proud of myself for being proactive. Next, I decided to pamper myself and took a long hot bath and relaxed for the evening. I watched a little television and fell asleep. I wanted to be refreshed for the next day because I had planned to go to Alcatraz and have dinner at the Pier.

When I awoke the next morning, I called room service for breakfast. I finished my coffee and bagel and still needed to jump in the shower just to wake up. I was dressed and out of the door so I could make the first afternoon tour to Alcatraz. It would be my first time crossing a body of water. Normally, if it was too much water for me to drink I would be nowhere near it. I took a terrified beginners swimming lesson as a young adult

A Mother's Influence

and needless to say I didn't learn how to swim and I'm still terrified. I'm going to blame it on the instructor; she wasn't a very good teacher. I think she had allowed too many people to take the class and she was not paying attention when I went under the water and had to be resuscitated. However, I knew the only way I was going to get to Alcatraz was to take the Blue and Gold Fleet across the San Francisco Bay. My desire to see a piece of history outweighed my fear.

Even though the boat ride wasn't as bad as I'd feared, I couldn't wait to get off the boat. I told myself to just take in the historical ambience. I felt like the boat ride was a part of being on Alcatraz because I couldn't escape and I was surrounded by a body of water. Alcatraz had been turned into a National Park. We were given a guided tour, and also heard recordings of the history of Alcatraz. I'd done my research and found out that the prison housed a lot of dangerous felons. At one time, it had been a military prison and a federal prison. It was the home of Al "Scarface" Capone and George "Machine Gun" Kelly, as well as many other notorious felons. I remember walking in one of the cells and standing there for a minute, trying to imagine how they lived in such confined quarters for as many as twenty five years. There was very little of civilization that you could see from Alcatraz. *Freedom is so precious, I thought, how could one just blatantly give it up so vicariously.* Alcatraz was a concrete fortress surrounded by water. The guards and their families lived on the island and the only way to get in and out was by boat. The children had to take a boat to school every day unless the water was too choppy to travel or the weather was bad. All of the supplies were also shipped in by boat or some type of barge. Everyone on the island was confined. The prison was shut down in 1963 because it had become too costly to maintain. I did a lot of walking, it was a huge facility and I wanted to see every nook and cranny. I barely remember the ride back because I was thinking how someone could survive in captivity for twenty or more years after enjoying the freedoms that we were born with and exposed to.

A Mother's Influence

Once I returned from my excursion from Alcatraz, I decided to have dinner at Pier 39. It was just as historical as the rest of the places I'd been. I could smell the fresh seafood in the air. I was trying to decide whether to go to a restaurant or stop at a street vender and get a sourdough bowl of clam chowder. I started with the chowder and decided I couldn't leave this city without having a fresh lobster dinner with all the fixings. I looked around for a restaurant and decided to stand in the longest line because the desk clerk had mentioned that restaurant. I made a mental note to thank the desk clerk because he knew exactly what he was talking about. My eyes were bigger than my stomach and I ended up taking most of my dinner back to the hotel with me.

As I was walking back to my hotel, my cell phone rang and it was David. He asked me if I'd made it home safely and I dreaded telling him that I was in San Francisco because I knew if I'd told him he would have wanted to be with me. He told me how much he was missing me and still hoped that I would consider his proposal. I ignored what he'd said and told him that

I was really tired and would talk with him later. When I got up

to my room I put the remainder of my meal in the refrigerator

and told myself, *I have breakfast for tomorrow.* I took a quick

shower, got into the bed and fell asleep.

I woke up well rested and ready for another full day of

sightseeing. I was anxiously looking forward to driving across

the Golden Gate Bridge. I'd seen the bridge by sea when I went

to Alcatraz and now I was about to experience it by land. As I

approached the bridge, I began to get a little nervous. I noticed

that there were several lanes of traffic on each side of the

median, with no real divider. I told myself to drive very

cautiously and pay attention to others. I didn't want to be the

person to cause a major accident. I briefly forgot about those

thoughts and began taking in the breathtaking views. Crossing

the bridge took me less than ten minutes. I got off the bridge

and headed to Sausalito.

A Mother's Influence

Sausalito was a small quaint town. I found a place to park surrounded by the picturesque waterfront. Being in Sausalito was the closest I'd come to being in paradise. It had gorgeous views. You could see hills and beaches and the streets were filled with little quaint restaurants, museums, art shop and street entertainers. It was breathtaking. I immediately told myself that I'd like to come back one day with the love of my life to experience everything that the town had to offer. I wanted to take it all in, the hiking trails, the bike rides, and the boating. I sat at one of the outside cafes, drinking a glass of wine and just taking in the breathtaking views and daydreaming. It was just a great day to be alive and I sat there thanking God for his many blessings. I did manage to order lunch. I was so deep in thought I hadn't realized that I'd been there for two hours. I told myself the next time I came to visit this town, I would stay a few days and relax and take in the beauty of everything that Sausalito had to offer.

I realized if I wanted to take the drive to Napa, I would need to get on the road and drive for a couple of hours. I didn't stop along the way; I just wanted to take in the scenery and the fall foliage. The views were exquisite; the vibrant orange, gold's and crimson so very vivid. Looking up at the hills reminded me of the words to the Sound of Music.

When I got back to the hotel that evening, I was drained and ordered room service again. I took a hot shower and realized that I had one more day left in San Francisco. Before going to bed, I read the story of Chinatown from the pamphlet that I'd gotten in the hotel lobby. It was very intriguing. I told myself that I'd wake up early and head to Chinatown. *I can't believe the time has gone by so fast. It seems like only yesterday I was flying into San Francisco with plenty of time to spare.*

Who would have thought that at ten o'clock in the morning, I would find myself standing under the arch that says "Welcome to Chinatown." I realized that today was my last day and tonight when I go back to the hotel, I would spend my evening packing and wishing I had more time to spend in this beautiful city.

Chinatown was a wonderful escape. There were people speaking different dialects. It was almost like being transported to another country. You could see pagoda roofs; it felt as if I had traveled to Asia. Standing in Chinatown just looking around I was in sensory overload with the sights of the brilliant colors and smells. As I walked down the sidewalks, I was trying to take it all in. I browsed in storefronts that had clothes hanging everywhere. There were some stores that had racks and racks of meat hanging from the rafters. There were all types of fruits, vegetables and spices that I'd not heard of. It awakened all of my senses. I saw all different brands of teas and I bought at least five different types to try and to give away as gifts for my tea - drinking friends. One of my last stops was to visit the Golden Gate Fortune Cookie Factory where some twenty thousand cookies are made a day by two women. One of the ladies handed me a sample fortune cookie. I was anxious to read my fortune. As I pulled it from the cookie, it read, "Love never dies. It might dim but never goes out." As usual, I had dessert before my meal.

I decided to stop in an authentic Chinese restaurant for what would probably be one of my last meals in San Francisco and decided to try Dim Sum, which was a variety of all types of food. Everything I tasted was delicious. I thought, *another doggie bag.* As I was sitting in the restaurant alone, I couldn't help but reflect on how Chinatown reminded me of Ellis Island. It was also built and developed by people who immigrated to this country in search of opportunities for a better way of living, Chinatown on the west coast and Ellis Island on the east coast.

As I was leaving Chinatown, I could just imagine how it must look at night with colorful paper lanterns hanging everywhere. This had been a vacation that I'll remember for a lifetime. I headed back to my hotel to pack and get ready for an early morning flight back to reality.

When I returned to Buffalo, it felt unfamiliar because I'd been gone for so long and so much had happened to me. I took a long nap. When I woke up, I decided to check the answering machine. There was a call from Samantha welcoming me back home and a call from David still professing his love for me. Feelings of sadness and anxiousness came over me. *I should probably write him a letter*, I thought. I knew I had to take the time to explain that I wasn't in love with him and my heart had been taken a long time ago. The love he had for me reminded me of the love I had for Ryan. I told myself, *One day, I'll have to face Ryan again.*

Chapter Ten

It had been a while, but Ryan and I had managed to keep in touch from time-to-time. Over the years, we'd seen each other a time or two. We would always call each other on holidays and special occasions. Ryan would sometimes send cards just to say, *thinking of you.*

One day, I started to reflect on my life and decided I still loved Ryan and I was being foolish to stay away from him just because I feared he would break my heart again. I decided to call him, which was out of character for me. Ryan would always say, "Anolese, I'm so happy to hear your voice. I've been thinking about you." That was his phrase almost every time I called him. I knew I would probably have to tell him exactly what was on my mind, because I'd told him a long time ago that we'd never have a future together after he remarried his ex-wife.

A Mother's Influence

I told Ryan I had made plans to visit my parents for Thanksgiving and it would be nice if we could see each other.

Ryan reluctantly said, "Anolese, I will be out of town visiting my son who's moved to Jamaica."

I told him that I understood that everyone at this time of the year wanted to be with their families. "Have fun, I said, "and maybe we will chat later during the holidays."

Ryan said, "Anolese, I look forward to it. Maybe we can get together before the end of the year?" We hung up the phone. *I've always loved the way he says my name,* I thought.

I took off the three days before Thanksgiving and flew home to visit my parents. My cousin, Anna, picked me up at the airport. She was my favorite first cousin. She always made time for me and we spent the first day of my trip hanging out together. She had two beautiful children I adored. Although it was a long drive, Anna would make the trip to Canton to take me home. She never wanted our visit to end. She lived in

Dahlonega, Georgia which was almost two hours from where my parents lived.

Dad always purchased a ham from the Virginia Baked Ham store a few days before Thanksgiving. Secretly, I don't think Dad thought Mama was a very good cook and I know he missed Grandma's cooking.

I enjoyed cooking in the kitchen with my Mama. Mama made the best potato salad I've ever tasted. She would always put apples, fresh pecans, pimentos, red and green peppers, celery and a few other spices that she kept as a secret. Mama always cooked enough food for an army just in case friends or relatives stopped by. I loved Thanksgiving because it never came on a Sunday, which always gave us a longer weekend. We would get up early in the morning and skip breakfast because we knew we would be eating early. Mama wasn't into decorating the table, except for a tablecloth. She always asked one of us kids to set the table. I, on the other hand, went outside to pick up leaves and pine cones to decorate the table. I would place them around the table to give it a festive vibe. You could barely see the table decorations due to all the food on the table. Mama also had additional dishes on the kitchen table. Most times, she would invite over other relatives and we kids would have to eat at a card table. We didn't care. It just meant we could eat whatever we wanted and as much as we wanted. By the time we got up from the table, we were stuffed. I enjoyed the dark meat of the turkey but Mama also cooked fried chicken, fried okra and fried corn which was also some of my favorites. During the holidays, no one worried about overeating. You could find the relatives lingering around the house, napping for hours, before having leftovers. We kids would go out and play to make room for dessert.

Thanksgiving was one of the best days of the year, with the exception of Christmas. Growing up, we were always around family and friends. The laughter was exhilarating. We would always have such a good time. I had such good memories as a kid, playing board games, and visiting friends and family. During the Christmas holidays, Dad would put all of us kids in the car and drive through various neighborhoods to see the Christmas lights. My weekend holiday ended too soon.

Before I knew it, the time had come for me to return to Buffalo. I hated leaving my family, but I had made a life for myself in upstate New York. I tried to continue the family traditions from my childhood. Due to work, I could not go home again for Christmas. Besides, the weather was always so unpredictable, which made it difficult to plan. I would always try to make the best of the holidays in Buffalo.

I had boxes and boxes of Christmas decorations that I would normally put out every year. This year, I was slightly depressed and knew I would be alone, as I had just spent Thanksgiving with my family and those memories flooded my mind and made me both happy and sad. I'd bought presents early for my niece and nephews and mailed them. This year, I was not in the mood to decorate and go all out for Christmas. I needed a distraction, so I decided to call Ryan. I remembered what he'd said about the possibility of seeing each other before the end of the year.

I called Ryan and he said, "Anolese, I'm so happy to hear your voice. I've been thinking about you."

I asked him if he had any plans for Christmas and he said, "Not exactly." I saw this as an opportunity to invite him to Buffalo. His first reaction was how cold it was here at this time of the year. I immediately thought, *He's no longer interested in me.* I also told myself, *No negative thinking.*

Ryan said, "Maybe it's time for me to come and play in the snow. I would like to come to Buffalo for a White Christmas."

I was shocked and didn't know what to say next.

Ryan said, "Anolese, did you hear me?"

I heard him, but I wanted him to say it once more. Ryan said, "Anolese, I have a very short timeframe but I'll be there for Christmas."

I couldn't believe what I was hearing. I was so happy.

Ryan said, "Anolese, I'll call you in a few days to let you know what arrangements I've made."

I was still in shock.

Ryan said, "Anolese are you still there?"

I said, "Yes, Ryan. I'll await your phone call." When I got off the phone, I started making all kinds of plans for Christmas.

I had to sit still for a moment and replay the conversation back in my head. I looked up and said, "Thank you God, my prayers had been answered." I screamed aloud, "Yes, he's coming for Christmas!" I picked up the phone to call Samantha, but she wasn't home. I left her a message to call me immediately. I didn't want the message to frighten her, but I was overjoyed. I called my sister and said, "Guess who's coming for Christmas?"

"Ryan? Oh thank God, I'm so happy for you."

After the phone call with my sister, I started pulling out the boxes of decorations I didn't think would be touched this year. About an hour into unpacking Christmas decorations and placing them throughout the house, the doorbell rang.

I went to the door and opened it. Samantha was standing there with a look of concern. "Anolese, what's wrong? I got home and got your message and tried to call you but your phone has been busy. I decided to drive over. What's wrong?"

I told Samantha that I didn't mean to frighten her, but that I had some good news.

Samantha said, "Well, don't keep it to yourself. What is it?"

I told her that Ryan was coming for Christmas.

Her face went from a look of anticipation to despair. Samantha immediately said, "If he disappoints you again, I'll fly to Atlanta and put a hurt on him."

I told her that my sister had said the very same thing but she wasn't so polite.

Samantha told me that she was going home and would be back in a few days to help me finish my decorations.

"Samantha when you come back, you might be able to help me decorate the trees. Everything else will be done."

Samantha said, "Before I leave, I need to sit down and sip a glass of wine to calm my nerves. You scared the mess out of me. Anolese, I'm happy and will be there for you because you're my best friend and I love you. However, I'm also concerned. I can't forget all the times that he's disappointed

A Mother's Influence

you. Ryan doesn't have a good track record. I know this isn't

what you wanted to hear, but I had to get that off my chest."

After she went home, I thought about what Samantha

said. But I had to go out on this limb again.

Like every other year, I couldn't have a fresh cut tree

due to my allergies. I always put up at least three trees. A large

tree adorned the living room with nothing but angels, gold

ribbon, gold bulbs and stars. It was my favorite tree. The tree

that I had in my family room was decorated with Santa's that I'd

collected over the years. The tree in my bedroom was not as

elaborate, but was very special. It was decorated with

ornaments that my friends had given me over the years.

Just think...twenty four hours ago I had no reason to

decorate and now Ryan is coming. The excitement

overwhelmed me. Over the years, I always felt alone after

friends and family had left my house on Christmas Eve. That

would not be the case this year because Ryan would be here and I was jubilant.

My heart was racing from the excitement of the day. I decided that I'd take a nice long bubble bath and try to calm down. I felt the way I did when I was a young girl waiting for Santa to arrive with much anticipation. After the bath, I still couldn't fall asleep. I had too much on my mind. I needed to get up and make a list of all the things I needed to accomplish before Christmas, which was only three weeks away.

I went from room-to-room trying to picture where my decorations would look best. I decided that when Ryan arrived, I'd put his luggage in the guest room. It would be too presumptuous of me to think he would want to sleep with me on the first night, or any night for that matter. We really didn't have that type of a relationship.

As I was standing in the guest room, I decided that it needed to be spruced up. It had been the catch-all room. I cleaned the room and decided to purchase new linens. *And I probably need to buy a new blanket to keep Ryan warm.* I cleaned out the closet, so he would have a place to put his clothes. I finally felt exhausted enough to sleep.

The next morning, I woke up with joy in my heart. I skipped breakfast to continue sprucing up the house. When I finally finished, the guest room looked elegant as did the rest of the house.

I called Samantha and told her that I'd just purchased a new pre-lit Christmas tree and I was going to decorate it the next day.

Samantha immediately said, "Make strawberry daiquiris and I'll be there after work."

I told her I would only make a small pitcher because I needed her to assist me with the tree. "And you know how you are when you drink."

That evening, when we finished decorating the tree, it looked gorgeous with the many different black angels that I'd collected over the years. It had gold bulbs, stars, little plaques that said peace, love, joy and hope. It had a black angel tree topper. The gold skirt around the tree matched the stockings that were hung on the mantel. Everything was perfect. The time had gone by so fast. It was almost two weeks until Christmas.

I decided to fill a stocking for Ryan. I bought three pairs of socks, Passion cologne for men - because it was my favorite - and a variety of other items. I didn't want him to feel bad in case he didn't buy me anything. Samantha called me and asked me if I wanted to go shopping with her. I told her she must have been reading my mind. "Samantha, I was thinking about how Ryan hates the cold weather and I wanted to get him a heavy sweater."

After we'd been in the store browsing for a few hours, I found the perfect thick heavy sweater and I was ready to go.

A Mother's Influence

This must have been the beginning of Samantha's shopping because she was on a buying spree and she had a list. I told Samantha, "Rome wasn't built in a day. The mall will still be here tomorrow." I'd already purchased gifts for the rest of my family and most of them were already in the mail. I couldn't wait to get home and wrap Ryan's gift.

Samantha and I decided to stop at Friendly's and get a bite to eat. I loved their Strawberry Fribble, which is like a frozen milkshake. I could take a milkshake over food any day of the week and that's what I ordered. Samantha started to question me on the details of when Ryan would arrive. Before I answered her question, I realized that I'd not heard from him in two weeks, which was unusual. An uneasy feeling came over me and I snapped at her. I told her, "Ryan will probably let me know in a day or two, if he needs me to pick him up or whether he's going to rent a car. Knowing Ryan, he's probably going to surprise me." However, I knew in the back of my mind that something was wrong. I thought, *am I going to be disappointed again?* After snapping at Samantha, she didn't say another word. I think Samantha could sense what I was thinking about and she didn't want to push the issue.

When Samantha dropped me off, my mood had changed. I dreaded what I knew I had to do next. I had to call Ryan. I felt in my heart that something was wrong. I stopped to say a little prayer and then I picked up the phone and dialed his number. Ryan answered on the first ring.

"Hi Ryan, I'm planning my grocery list for the week and I wanted to make sure I had some of your favorite foods on hand. What would you like to snack on?"

There was a moment of silence. Ryan said, "I'm not coming."

I was stunned. I thought, *Maybe I didn't understand what he just said.* I asked, "What did you say?"

Ryan said again, "I'm not coming because it'll cost too much money."

I said, "You told me that money was no object. What's the real reason?"

He quietly said, "My son came over today and talked me into going to the Southern Bowl game with him and his brother the day after Christmas. Besides, it's too cold in Buffalo at this time of the year."

I told Ryan, "Make sure you tell your sons the pain they caused in breaking one promise to make another. On second thought, don't tell them anything. It's not their fault, it's yours. They're old enough to understand that you'd made a prior arrangement."

I immediately had a flashback to the time I'd been at my lowest point, when I'd considered committing suicide after Ryan told me he was going to remarry his ex-wife. I was so mad at myself because I'd let him in again and trusted him. I asked him if he'd told his sons that he'd made other arrangements. "How could you disappoint me like this? How could you ruin my Christmas? I've made all kinds of plans based on the fact you were spending Christmas with me."

"Ryan, when were you going to tell me that you'd changed your mind?"

Ryan responded "Anolese, I was going to tell you Sunday."

I replied, "Sunday, a few days before Christmas? How could you?" I was so upset. I tried to hold back the tears, but I couldn't. Even if he couldn't see my tears, I'm sure he could hear them in my voice. I hung up the phone and cried my eyes out. I was devastated, disappointed and too ashamed to tell my friends that I was played for a fool again and that Ryan wasn't coming. I decided that for only one evening, I was going to feel sorry for myself and tune out the world. After all those counseling sessions, I was not going to let myself sink that low ever again.

It was the next day when Samantha called me to see if I was attending the office party that evening. I quickly said, "No!" I told Samantha that I didn't feel well, but Samantha's last words were, "I'll see you there." I knew if I didn't attend, Samantha would worry about me.

I started to get dressed for the party. I was hoping Samantha would not mention my plans for Christmas. After a couple of drinks, I felt free enough to sing my sad song once again. I decided to tell Samantha what had happened. Samantha reacted just as I expected, being a true friend who was really pissed. She wanted Ryan's phone number. I wouldn't give it to her, as she'd already called him a few choice names in my presence. I'd tuned out most of her conversation, but I knew she cared about me and my feelings and that's why she was so angry.

A Mother's Influence

I left the party around nine o'clock that evening and all I wanted to do was go home and go to bed. I just wanted to go to sleep, so the pain would go away. I'd promised myself that around my friends, I would act as if Ryan's not coming for Christmas didn't bother me. It was just another one of the many disappointments that I had to bear.

I started to cry, as I began to remember all the fantasies that I'd played out around our reunion. As I drifted deep in thought, I imagined Ryan coming to Buffalo to be here with me for Christmas and having a wonderful time. I imagined that he'd been so in love with me that he'd had made elaborate plans with my friends to meet him at a restaurant, so he could propose to me again in front of my friends. There would be no doubt he loved me. *How could I have been so stupid?*

I finally realized that I'd been carrying on a mental affair with the man I'd loved all these years in my head. It was clear to me now by his actions that I didn't mean the same to him.

A Mother's Influence

Ryan had hurt me just like so many others had done in the past. I finally began to realize that I'd been living a fantasy I created and nurtured in my mind for over twenty years.

Ryan was able to move beyond our tender beginnings, while I was still locked in my childhood fantasy. He'd made a life for himself without me and it seemed as if he'd wanted it to remain that way. I knew life was too short to live in the past. Ryan was making it clear that I needed to begin the healing process again and move on. My heart was telling me that he still loved me but something was wrong. *I can't wait any longer for the ice around Ryan's heart to thaw.* It didn't really matter what I thought. *I just need to move on.*

Chapter 11

Christmas had been such a disappointment for me in respect to Ryan ditching me at the last minute. I'd longed to be with Ryan, but he'd disappointed me again. I knew New Year's Day was approaching and I dreaded being alone for yet another holiday. I decided to put the past behind me and get on with my life. In six more days, it would be a new year and I prayed every day for a change in my life. I asked God to make this year better than the last one.

I had grown up to believe you shouldn't clean on New Year's Day. I spent two days before New Year's Day doing chores. My mother was very superstitious about certain things and of course her superstitions were passed on to me. I made sure that everything in the house was clean. The clothes were washed and I'd gotten all of my chores done. I took clothes to the cleaners and I did my grocery shopping. Mama would

A Mother's Influence

always say the way the house looked on New Year's Day is the way you'll keep it all year. As kids, we always had to clean the house and make sure all the clothes were washed and there were no dirty dishes in the sink. Mama would say, "If you wash on New Year's Day, you might wash someone out of the family." In Mama's mind, everything had to be spotless. That's why I started my cleaning rituals two days before. By the time New Year's Eve arrived, all I had to do was take a nice long bubble bath and prepare to bring in a new beginning. Most New Year's Eves, I would go to church. But since the weather was so bad, I didn't want to chance being out on the roads late at night in a snowstorm all by myself.

It was five o'clock on New Year's Eve. When I looked out the door, I noticed that the driveway looked as if it had not been shoveled in days. I figured it could wait a little while longer. I wasn't going out again and I wasn't expecting any company. Later that evening, I started to cook myself dinner. I made grilled tilapia and a salad. After having dinner and cleaning the kitchen, I decided to pamper myself. I ran water in the tub and decided to take a nice long bubble bath. I rubbed my body with my favorite scented lotion. I looked in the closet and found the new nightgown that I'd purchased for myself for Christmas. It was almost nine o'clock, and I decided to get ready for bed. It had been a long day. I was going to do everything in my power to try to stay awake and greet the first day of the rest of my life. I had a bottle of Asti Spumante wine in the fridge and I decided to pour myself a glass and leave it next to my bedside table to toast in the New Year. I turned on the TV, so I could watch Dick Clark's New Year's Eve Show. I wanted to watch the ball drop. I turned the TV down low and I set my bed side clock to wake me up just minutes before the approaching New Year in case I fell asleep. My eyes were probably closed before my head hit the pillow. I woke up abruptly. I didn't know if I'd heard a noise, or if I'd dreamt that I heard something. I lay there very still to try to convince myself that I was dreaming. Moments later, I heard the doorbell. It frightened me. I looked over at the clock and noticed that it was thirty minutes before midnight. I turned on my bedside table lamp and got out of the bed. I put on my robe, walked out into the hallway and turned on the light. I walked down the stairs and was very happy that I had a peephole. I looked out the peephole and saw a man walking toward a taxi. I opened the door because I was still protected by another locked glass entry door. The taxi driver motioned to the man that I was standing in the doorway.

My heart was pounding. I stood there for a moment paralyzed, I couldn't move. It was Ryan. He said, "I was about to leave. I didn't think you were home." He walked back to the cab and handed the driver money, turning back to face me. "Are you going to let me in, sweetie?"

I managed to ask, "Ryan, what are you doing here?"

Ryan said again, "Are you going to let me in?" As I opened the door, Ryan dropped his luggage and hugged me for a long time. Ryan said, "Can you ever forgive me for disappointing you? I'm so sorry."

I stood there looking at him, wondering what happened between Christmas and New Year's. Ryan said, "Anolese, I was sitting home earlier today thinking about you and I just decided to drive to the airport and catch the first flight to Buffalo. I know I didn't call you, but I was willing to stay in a hotel until I was able to see you. I have spent most of my life confused."

I said, "About what?"

Ryan said, "I'll tell you later. I've always known I loved you. I have never been able to be completely honest with you or myself. Anolese, I woke up this morning with you on my mind and I knew for the first time in my life that I didn't want to spend another moment without you."

I was so happy to finally hear those words and be in the arms of the man I loved. I loved him with all my heart and finally I knew he loved me. As I walked back to my bedroom

A Mother's Influence

with Ryan by my side, I sat down on the bed and poured a second glass of Asti for Ryan. It was one minute to midnight and we toasted the New Year in together. The timer on my television turned off the TV and hour later and the room went dark.

Ryan began to kiss and caress me. I felt the ice melting. I helped him take off his clothes and threw them over a chair.

When the sun came up the next morning, we were exhausted from talking and making passionate love. We'd been awake all night. We were both too fatigued to make breakfast, so we slept most of the day. When we finally decided to get up around two o'clock that afternoon, Ryan asked me if there were any stores open. I told him that Wal-Mart and Wegman's were open. He asked me, "What is Wegman's?" I told him that it was a grocery store which had a little of everything. Ryan must have known that he could probably find what he needed at Wegman's. I asked him what he needed and he said, "A few personal items." I decided not to ask too many questions. I gave my car keys to him and told him to use the GPS in the car and to call me if he needed me. I told Ryan that I'd have brunch ready when he returned.

I was busy setting the table and preparing our meal. I cut up fresh fruit, strawberries, pineapple, bananas and watermelon to make a fresh fruit cocktail. I had already fried the bacon and was waiting for Ryan to return to make his eggs. The bagels were sliced and ready to toast. I was trying to decide whether to put out cream cheese or butter. I heard Ryan when he returned and I yelled out that I was in the kitchen. I heard him as he walked down the hall to my bedroom and closed the door. A few minutes later, I told him that breakfast was ready.

Ryan said, "Anolese, come here. I need your assistance." When I opened the bedroom door, Ryan was on one knee with rose petals all over the room. He said, "Anolese, will you marry me? I know daisies are your favorite flowers, but they're not in season."

I hesitated for a few minutes; I was just trying to take it all in. I said, "Ryan, are you serious? Do you really want to marry me? We've been through this before and it ended badly."

Ryan said, "Anolese, if you say yes, we'll get married before I leave to go home. I don't want to wait."

I finally said, "Yes, Ryan, yes, I'll marry you."

Chapter 12

I told Ryan that I wanted a big wedding. Ryan and I celebrated our life together that day and the next day. We spent many hours talking. Ryan had been in Buffalo four days before I told my best friends that I needed them to come over, that I had a surprise for them. When they arrived, they were speechless when I finally introduced them to Ryan. I told them that Ryan and I were going to get married. My friends looked skeptical and shocked. However, they were very cordial to him.

When I walked them out, they asked me if I was crazy. Samantha said, "Anolese, have you lost your mind? Have you forgotten this is the man who's caused you so much pain? He's disappointed you on so many occasions. You nearly committed suicide over this man. Are you losing your mind?"

I know they wanted what was best for me and they all commented on how happy I seemed, but they wondered how long it would last. As my friends left, I could see them outside talking among themselves. I knew they were probably saying things like, "he's going to hurt her again." But I knew this time would be different.

Ryan stayed a few days longer, so we could plan our lives together. When it was time for Ryan to leave, I didn't want him to go. I had gone without him for so long. I really didn't want him out of my sight. We got to the airport, parked the car and I went in with him. Ryan checked in and walked back toward me. We held each other for at least ten minutes. He continued to confess his love to me and me to him, and we finally let each other go. I talked to him before he got on the plane and when he got off the plane and every day until our wedding day.

I went back to work the following week and gave my supervisor a month's notice. My supervisor looked at me in dismay and asked, "Anolese, what's wrong? Why are you leaving?"

I told James that I was moving back to Georgia to get married.

James said, "I didn't know you were engaged. I didn't know you were seeing anyone." He caught himself asking personal questions and stopped.

I looked at him and said, "I'm marrying my childhood sweetheart."

James said, "Congratulations, you'll be missed."

I called my realtor and put my house on the market. Samantha, Susan and Elisa tried to talk me out of selling my house, but I did it anyway. I had scheduled my wedding for March twelfth. My friends had all agreed to drive down to Georgia with me for the wedding. I'd been consumed with the preparation of leaving my job, selling my house and planning my wedding. I talked with Ryan on the phone every day. My friends were so afraid that something would go wrong, but they tried not to show it. I was so happy that even if they'd shown their fears, it would not have mattered to me. I was in love and I knew in my heart that I'd be with Ryan for the rest of my life. All of my friends had taken the week off to drive to Georgia to help me prepare for the glorious event.

My friends and I left the same day the moving van left. We were headed to what they all hoped would be the happiest day of my life. It took two days to get there. We spent the night in a hotel, stopping several times for gas, food and shopping. I'd picked out a simple but elegant wedding dress. I decided that since all of my girlfriends were married, they would all be matrons of honor. We arrived in Atlanta two days after leaving Buffalo and went directly to Ryan's apartment. When I knocked on the door, Ryan's brother, Brad, greeted us. Brad looked at me with sadness in his eyes and said that Ryan was in the hospital. Brad said, "Why don't you guys follow me to the hospital."

Chapter 13

As we drove to the hospital, I was a nervous wreck; a thousand thoughts went through my mind. My friends and I went into Ryan's room.

Ryan turned to greet me and said, "Hi, sweetie."

I said, "Hi, honey."

My girlfriends all left the room.

Anolese, "When I was there in January, I told you that I had cancer but it was in remission. It was the same cancer my mother died from. I know that was no reason to stay away from you all those years, but I didn't want to burden you."

"Ryan, we don't have to go over this conversation again. I told you that the only thing that matters is that we're together again. I understand you were afraid, but you didn't have to look at it as a burden for me to bear. I never would have looked at it that way. Marriage is being with someone through sickness and health. I hated thinking all those years that you didn't love me, but I also understand that things don't happen in our time, they happen in God's time. He's seen fit for us to live the rest of our lives together, no matter how much time we have together."

"Anolese, I didn't have the heart to let you know my cancer had returned. It's inoperable. I was hoping I'd have more time to spend with you, but it's has gotten worse. The doctor will be in soon to talk with you, but I don't believe we have much time left."

"Ryan, I will be by your side, no matter how little time we have left. I'll never leave you and I'll cherish every moment that God allows us to be together."

"Anolese, I didn't have the heart to let you know my cancer had returned and it's inoperable. I was hoping I'd have more time to spend with you, but its gotten worse." Due to the effects of Ryan's illness, he was unaware of his repetitiveness.

A Mother's Influence

My friends came back into the room once Brad had updated them on Ryan's situation. I did not initially see them until I turned from Ryan, as he'd drifted to sleep. I didn't want him to see the tears that were forming in my eyes. I spotted my friends behind me and they were also trying to keep it together. We walked outside his room for a couple of seconds. I told them I wasn't going to leave his side, but they could stay at Ryan's apartment. Brad would make sure they got back there.

When Ryan awoke, he reminded me that his cancer was hereditary; both his mother and his sister had died from the same type of cancer. He told me that was the reason he didn't want to come for Christmas. He knew that was my favorite holiday and he didn't want me to associate his illness with Christmas. Ryan said, "Anolese, I've caused you so much pain in your life. I didn't want you to have to endure this with me. I love you, but I was trying to protect you." Ryan said that New Year's Eve was when he'd decided, no matter how much time he had left, that he wanted to spend it with me.

I'd known all my life that I loved Ryan and, deep down inside, I'd known he loved me too. What I hadn't known was the reason for the avoidance. However, I realized after finding out, I understood why he'd disappointed me so many times.

I loved Ryan and I wanted to be with him, even if that meant for a few hours. I stayed by his bedside for five days. I was holding his hand when he took his last breath and passed away. Kara had been one of my closest childhood friends. She'd flown in for my wedding and found herself attending a funeral. My friends and I attended Ryan's funeral, they were my strength. I didn't think I could have gone through the excruciating pain I was feeling without them.

When we got back to Ryan's apartment, my friends were full of questions and sorrow. Samantha said, "Anolese, what are you going to do? You've sold your house and most of your belongings."

A Mother's Influence

I couldn't bring myself to answer that question at the time.

Susan said, "Anolese, I can't stand seeing you in this much pain."

All I could do was crawl up into a ball and cry. I just wanted to be left alone. I went to Ryan's bedroom to lie down. I could still smell his scent on the pillow. I went to his closet and put on one of his sweaters, and I finally fell asleep.

Early the next afternoon, the doorbell rang. It was Brad and both of Ryan's sons. As we all sat around the kitchen table, my friends feared the worse.

The boys started out by saying, "Anolese, we feel as if we've known you for a long time. Dad told us all about you. He told us that he never wanted to say anything that would disrespect our mom, but that he loved you. Dad said that you were his first love and he let you get away. He told us that later in life he met our mom and that we were his greatest

accomplishments."

I was speechless. I'd told myself for years that Ryan

didn't love me or care enough about me to come and find me.

But now, I knew that he had felt the same way I did. He was the

love of my life.

Chapter 14

However, I thanked God every day that he brought Ryan back into my life and that we had a brief but amazing time together. Brad said, "Anolese, we hate to bother you, but the boys would like a few of their father's things." Brad gave me a list and told me to take my time getting the things together. I told Brad I would give him a call, so he could come back and pick the items up.

Samantha had a strange look on her face and I could see that she couldn't wait for them to leave so that she could question me. When they finally left, Samantha said, "What was Brad talking about? This place belongs to those boys. I expected him to ask you when you're leaving."

I could tell that Elisa and Susan also had a puzzling look on their face as well. Elisa wasn't as loud and outspoken as Samantha and Susan.

Samantha said, "Anolese, you know we all have to leave in two days, so maybe we should help you look for the things that Brad and the boys wanted."

I managed to mumble, "That's fine."

Susan immediately got up and went to the closet to search for the items that the boys had requested. In doing so, she found a box. She started screaming from the bedroom, "Anolese, there's a gift box in here with your name on it. It is wrapped so pretty."

Samantha said, "Susan, just bring it to her."

We were also sitting in the family room at that time. I'd started to cry again when the boys left and Samantha was trying to console me. Susan walked into the room with the box. I told her that I wasn't in the mood to look in that box.

Susan said, "Anolese, you have to open it. Ryan would want you to."

A Mother's Influence

"Susan, if I open the box it will seem so final for me. My heart is not only broken, it has been shattered."

Susan said, "I'm curious. Can I open it?"

I said, "Okay."

I could see Susan diligently taking the card off the top of the box. She was removing the bow, trying to unwrap the box without tearing the paper. Susan handed the card to me and, after lifting the top off the box, she handed it to me. Susan said, "This should be a private moment between you and Ryan."

I gently took the box from her and placed it beside me. No one said a word for a few minutes. The only noise you could hear in the room was me crying softly. I'd promised Ryan that I would mourn his loss, but not fall completely apart.

There were two boxes inside the big box. Inside the smaller box were our wedding bands. My band was engraved, "To the woman I have loved all of my life." I started to cry louder and harder. It was hard for me to catch my breath. At that moment, I realized I would have to live without the man I loved for the rest of my life and that I would never ever see him again. No more phone calls, no more passionate kisses; being held in the middle of the night, that sense of protection; it was all gone.

I opened the next box. There was a letter addressed to me, along with documents in the box. I opened the letter and read it. I put the letter on the table and went out on the balcony for some fresh air.

Samantha followed me. She said, "You know we love you and will always be here for you."

When I returned to the room, Susan asked, "Anolese, can we read the letter?"

I told her to go ahead. Susan began to read the letter aloud:

A Mother's Influence

My Dear Anolese,

If you are reading this letter, I am no longer here. I had planned to tell you all the things in this letter, but I wrote them down just in case. I want you to know that I have loved you most of my life. You have brought me so much joy these last couple of months. I feel like the most blessed man in the world when you married me on January 5th. I know for your friends, our wedding day will be April 30th. I wasn't about to leave Buffalo without you knowing the whole story and marrying you. It was so nice of the courthouse to rush our marriage license. God blessed us by allowing us to conceive a baby on our wedding night. The greatest joy for me was when we found out it was a little girl that we could name Jennifer. I know a man is not supposed to cry, but I can't stop crying because I am so happy. It has taken me twenty plus years, but I finally got my baby back. I can still picture the very first time I met you. I was washing my Volvo and I turned my water hose in your direction just to ensure we would have a conversation. You made a sarcastic comment and walked away. By that time, I was

intrigued and wanted to find out who you were. I quickly dried

the car and tried to follow you, but you were out of sight and I

didn't know which way you had gone. I saw one of my buddies

standing in front of the barber shop and asked him if he had

seen two girls walking by. Joe said, "Brenda and Anolese?" I

said, "I guess. What were they wearing?" "Brenda had on

shorts and Anolese had on a yellow dress." I said to myself, "Ah

hah, I know her name now. Anolese, I like the sound of that." I

started to blurt out all sorts of questions. "Do you know

Anolese? Where does she live?" He said she lives on Black

Creek Blvd. That was all I needed to hear. As I drove down

your street, I saw you sitting on a yellow swing on your front

porch and I waved. I awoke early the next morning and all I

could think about was you. I decided to change my jogging

route, so I could get a glimpse of you every day. When I passed

your house, I tried to imagine which room was yours. I wanted

to get to know you and would do anything to make that happen.

A Mother's Influence

When I saw you downtown one day carrying your books, I knew it was my chance to get to know you. Your voice lit up my heart. I can remember the first time I kissed you. It was after we had gone to the movies. I can't remember what we saw that evening, because my focus was always on you. I was on cloud nine and I said over and over to myself that you were the one I wanted to spend the rest of my life with.

Unfortunately, a chain of events kept us from being together, and we went our separate ways and made other lives for ourselves. I wanted to reach out to you many times, but I realized why you were reluctant to be with me after everything that I had put you through. When I found out that I had cancer and it was inoperable, I wanted to reach out to you, but I didn't think it was fair. I knew I only had a couple of years to live. I tried to reach out a few times when the cancer was in remission, but I could never follow through mainly because I was told I couldn't travel.

A Mother's Influence

On New Year's Eve, I realized that I would rather have two days with you than a few months by myself. I had to let you know how much you have meant to me for the last twenty years. I know that I got married and you and I went on with our lives, but I never forgot you. My two boys were my greatest loves and I told them about their sister, Jennifer. I have asked them to look out for you and their little sister.

Anolese, I will take you with me in my heart and my hope is that one day we will be together again. I love you with all my heart and don't you ever doubt that. If you are reading this letter without me, I want you to know that you are loved and I will take care of you forever. You are in my heart and you will always be with me. Please know that I never meant to hurt you.

In the other envelopes you will open, one will contain a deed to our new home. Please go by and see it with your girlfriends before they leave. It is my wedding present to you. I

A Mother's Influence

have also made sure that you and Jennifer will be taken care of

for the rest of your lives.

Much love, my darling, Anolese,

Your husband, Ryan.

I was still crying when I noticed that all of my friends were in tears, as well. As Susan finished reading the letter out loud, they were stunned. Samantha grabbed the box to search for the deed. Looking in the box, Samantha found the deed as well as a life insurance policy for two million dollars with my name as the beneficiary. Ryan had kept all of my letters and pictures.

Susan asked, "You really married him?"

Samantha said, "You're a widow? I can't believe you didn't tell us."

I was still crying. Samantha found a variety of cards Ryan had never sent.

A Mother's Influence

After being so overwhelmed with grief, we all decided we needed to take a drive and get out of the house for some fresh air. I had no idea that Samantha had Googled the address to the home that Ryan had purchased for me and Jennifer until we pulled into the driveway and Samantha said, "Anolese, you're home."

ACKNOWLEDGEMENTS

As I sit here with my thoughts, I am humbled and I thank God for the blessings he has bestowed upon me. I know it was God's mercy, grace, guidance and the angels that he put in my path that helped me get to where I am today.

There were many times that I said I needed help and every time I reached out to any of my friends they were there for me. It didn't matter if I wanted to read a paragraph, page, or a chapter to my friends in Georgia, New York, North Carolina or California they always listened. I thank my sister Angela for her constant encouragement. Michele, Raul and Glenn were my rocks, I don't know what I would have done without them. A special thanks goes out to Donita Cummings for always being my "friend, sister, and confident." We have gone through a lot together and will have a bond for life.

In my quest to write this book I felt as if God placed the crumbs of faith and hope to mark my path. I met people like Yvonne Thomas, CEO, Precision Creative Services, who introduced me to Dackeyia Q. Sterling, CEO/Publisher of Entertainment Power Players. Dackeyia, host of "Get Published for Real," without her guidance I would have been lost. I feel truly blessed.

I'd also like to thank the North Carolina Writers' Network for putting me in touch with Steven Manchester, the editor of my book as well as the author of many books.

I'd like to thank the rest of my siblings, "Barbara and Bobby," and the Gearing Family for helping to shape the person that I am today. May God continue to direct our path and watch over us.

36098135R00170

Made in the USA
Middletown, DE
24 October 2016